CIRCLE BACK

A Vital Novel by

Joey Kent

STORY MERCHANT BOOKS
LOS ANGELES

Circle Back

Copyright © 2024 by Joey Kent All rights reserved.

No part of this book may be reproduced or transmitted in any form or by any means without written permission of the author.

ISBN-13: 978-1-970157-52-9

Story Merchant Books
400 S. Burnside Avenue, #11B
Los Angeles, CA 90036
www.storymerchantbooks.com

www.529bookdesign.com

Also by Joey Kent

The Hayride Years by Frank Page with Joey Kent

Elvis: The Louisiana Hayride Years 1954–1956 by Frank Page with Joey Kent

Cradle of the Stars: KWKH & the Louisiana Hayride

Poetry in the Time of Coronavirus: The Anthology

Poetry in the Time of Coronavirus: Volume Two

The TCFFFV Poetry & Short Story Journal: Volume Seven

CIRCLE BACK

MARGARET:
SHALL WE WRITE THE
SEQUEL?!

Joey Kent 9/2/25

Für Elise

CIRCLE BACK

My darling Maezie,

In my youth, I prayed to God for you long before I ever knew you existed. I asked of my Savior that I may come to find a piece of me I sensed was missing; that I may come to know a singular and beautiful, deep and far-reaching, soul-altering experience that would prepare me in some way for the goodness of Heaven. Much sooner than I was prepared to handle, He sent you into my life—a beautiful dandelion whose blowball exploded all over my world when I proclaimed you perfect. I was totally blinded by your splendor and left searching for a way to repay the riches I was sure I did not deserve.

What you and I came to find in one another was divine, not of this Earth. And it came so easily that I failed to see its worth, failed to shield us from the routine attacks of this mortal world and our fragile human nature. When we collapsed under the strains and demands we'd placed on our union—on my watch!—I simply let it tear us apart. I have grieved every moment of every day of every decade since.

I was a boy charged with making the decisions of a man. I failed that man, and I failed you.

Maezie, my angel, what I could not know then, and what I've only recently come to see, is the rarest of love you and I shared those many years ago has continued to grow and mature in some otherworldly space. A great fog of misery rolled in and eclipsed our existence, or so we thought.

But what we grieved was never lost, only our ability to see it....

1
Maezie & Kenzie

Maezie. A name. A word, and in this case, a complete sentence—an expression of my heart that I know from the start of this opus I will fail, and fail miserably, to convey to you its deep, full, and complex meaning to me. I see it in print now, and I audibly gasp, as I have always done at any visual display or utterance of this moniker for my one true love in all of the universe, known and unknown. *Complete* is the adjective you should focus on and hold. Oh, yes, this is what we are dealing with. Maezie Fock is, and will always be, my everything.

Let us begin with the origin of the nickname of my beloved.

"Maezie" is a sing-song adaptation of Liesel Fock's middle name of Almay, which was not in the least any sort of fan tribute to the cosmetics line by her, shall we say, "unique" mother. No, likely Mother Belinda just wanted something soft abutting the offensive sounding Fock she'd been made through marriage to carry. Or, equally as likely, she simply recalled the name from some out-of-date, well-thumbed women's magazine at the beauty shop and later claimed it as her own invention.

Now, as to the spelling, further indulgence is required. One more typically spells such a name "Maisie" or some similar variant, but young Liesel Almay Fock would have none of that. Almost as soon as she grew out of MayMay, she was crowned Maisie by virtue of her own scribbled name on an—*I Love You, Mommy*—refrigerator art piece from when she was four. Upon further inspection of the lone survivor from the Mother's Day archive, this was followed by the cutest frown that only Maezie can, or ever could, make. It is part displeasure (like having encountered the flatulence from someone's processing of a plate of pork and beans), part pout, part cogitation, part wonder, and all joy in the eyes of the beholder. Maisie fancied herself somewhat of a country girl albeit—she determined at a remarkably early age—of the "refined" varietal.

Still, in that gentler era, the pretty country girls of the comics and the television seemed to be a "Mae" of some sort—Daisy Mae, Sally Mae, Fanny Mae, ad nauseam. So, on one ordinary day in second grade, Maisie drew another piece of art destined for the Norge, only this one depicted what was purported to be her daddy, Hubert S. Fock. The "S" stood for Shale, his daddy being a worker in an oilfield pipe yard without much inspiration for naming except this one effort when he'd lost all his lunch money throwing dice with the welders and had taken to smuggling a second, then third beer on what was left of his lunch break. And Hubert's mama didn't fight it, or just didn't give a shit. In later years, Maezie would swear to me often that the "S" was most assuredly for Stupid by virtue of the way she'd been treated during her odyssey of an upbringing. And, truth be known, "Hugh Stupid Fock" was a name we secretly favored often in our early courtship while we still discussed him at all.

Back to the art. I say it *purportedly* depicted her daddy, not to question her intentions but rather the execution of the piece that featured a blob and stick Hugh banging what looked to be a large wrench on the back of a square, black-and-white cow with stick legs beside the unmistakable red barn that still stands in sharp contrast to the brown, one-story sixties home along Route 9 in Uncertain, Texas. Hugh had a voice bubble above his head, which looked more like a balloon deflating in its haste to flee the scene. It simply said, "Git!" Whatever the reasoning or inspiration behind Liesel's artistic gift to her father that day, the only thing of significance was that she'd chosen to sign her name *Maezie*. Even then, little Liesel knew she would stand out in the world from that definitive moment on.

And thus, Liesel Almay was self-christened "Maezie" for evermore. No need to even deal with what her mother called "that hideous last name," so similar to the scandalous word that would all-too-soon be celebrated by the population at large as everything from a noun to a verb to an adjective and even a gerund. (I'll wait while you go look that one up and then recall it from seventh grade English class "oh, yeah....")

I view "Maezie" as a singular, wonderful name that's more than fine with me and makes my heart sing to this day.

• • •

Cell phones began their intrusion into my life toward the end of 2002. They were tiny back then, designed for making portable phone calls and not much else. Oh, there were soon instances of texting, if you were adept enough to get into the rhythm that was required to make words from the multiple letters assigned to the numbers on the dial pad. But why on earth would you text someone when you could simply call them and convey your message, however short or long? Text messages are, or should be, the "sticky notes" of today, quick fixes that can be written, sent, and removed once their purposes have been achieved. But they've become a way to honor the erosion of the average attention span by reducing all manner of vital conversations into a confusing shorthand of acronyms and emojis, each open to wide interpretation. Needless to say, texting was not my thing.

So, when it happened a few years back, my breathing had suddenly gone out of rhythm—I'm talking *way* out of rhythm—when I determined the unfamiliar Texas phone number that just pinged me belonged to my long-lost Maezie. I wasted no time creating a contact file to that number, then stood back and simply admired my handiwork. For the first time since I'd owned a cell phone, I was staring at that beautiful name on the display screen: *Maezie*.

Hot damn! Game on.

Hello, my friend. I got a message that you need me.

Maezie's carefully crafted response to the voice message I'd left at her work had been a classic understatement, for I had never needed anyone more. And I had never stopped needing this woman in particular.

"*Omnia vincit amor et nos cedamus amori!*" is how the Roman poet Virgil put it. "*Love conquers all; let us, too, yield to love!*" If you need an old Latin phrase to get your fires burning, well, by god that's a rather good one. But for Maezie and me, we could never control the looks, the giggles, the smiles, and the sheer joy of being with one another. We did more than yield, we merged full-on into love—it's safe to say love conquered us—and that's how this whole ordeal started.

2

Quito

I sat on a grand patio at the western edge of Murcielago Beach overlooking the Pacific Ocean in beautiful Manta, Ecuador, and picked through a healthy bowl of colorful melon balls, separating out the cantaloupe from the watermelon and the papaya and, what was that...guava? The Hotel Vistalmar is my refuge, and it is here on the tiled terrace where I took my breakfast under a large and billowy tree as the cool breeze coming off the ocean surrounded me with just the right amount of humidity. At first, it mattered that I taste each melon individually so that I could ascertain its full flavor and freshness and get to some common ground before simply stabbing the balls at random, adding in a slice of banana, and making up my own flavor combinations. I got carried away, though, and stuffed three or four into my mouth, drawing a smile from the ever-present Quito, who returned to check on me.

"The fruit is satisfying, no?" he asked the obvious question as I dabbed at the running juices on my chin and nodded in agreement.

"Yes, Quito. Thank you."

"More coffee?" he inquired, already guiding the pot toward my empty cup.

"God, yes!" I exclaimed to my surprise as much as anyone's. I love a good cup, but there was something unexpected in my morning jolt. "Is it the fruit or is the coffee...I don't know, sweet?"

"You are correct, señor. Ecuador is one of only fifteen countries in the world that produces both arabica and robusta coffee beans. We do not plant much, but what we do...." Quito finished his exacting pour, and I was treated to his friendly and welcoming smile.

I passed on the sugar and took another sip, this time to study more carefully.

"Peaches...and cream?"

"Oh, yes. Plums and apricots too. Gentle. Creamy. Floral. Not too acidic. Just the right fruity, yes? It is all there."

I nodded in agreement as I revisited my cup to affirm his running commentary. He was right, even if he said *app*-instead of *ape*-ricot. Quito had earned a pass.

"Is this some sort of specialty coffee?" I pressed my new friend.

"No, no. It is a shared hallmark of Ecuadorean coffee. You are enjoying Café Lissadale from right here in the

Manabí Province where the fields were first planted during the time of your Civil War."

"A hallmark, you say?" I like a man who uses big words and uses them properly. Quito nodded as he glanced to the only other occupied table on the pleasant veranda and gave a slight nod.

"You should be a tour guide, Quito," I joked with the man I barely knew.

"Oh, I am, señor, most afternoons."

"No shit?"

"Yes...or, rather, no. Whether your passion is coffee or chocolate, craft beer or our fine Panama hats—yes, they are made here—Quito can show you the world. All for a very reasonable price, I might add."

"Show me the world. I like that. Well, Quito, my passion actually arrives here in a few days, so, perhaps, we will avail ourselves of your knowledge and hospitality."

Quito flashed the smile, a heel click, a quick bow, and looked once more to the other occupied table.

"Go. Don't let me keep you from your job."

"I shall return with your eggs momentarily."

"Take your time." Quito nodded yet again as I offered a parting shot. "Just don't go too far with that coffee pot."

He turned his attention to servicing another guest and I returned mine to my cup of Café Lissadale. I don't often use extreme cuss words in my everyday vernacular, preferring to add them into my conversation as a "spice" in my own effort to preserve what little remains of their shock value in this day and age but, man! I had to say, even if it was to myself and under my breath, "That's some good fuckin' coffee."

This place really is spectacular. Manta, Ecuador. Not exactly where I imagined reconnecting with Maezie twenty-eight years after I last saw her, but I think she made an excellent choice for our upcoming rendezvous.

All I remember about Ecuador I learned from little Johnny Veenci when I was a kid, and he wasn't much more than a toddler. Johnny's mom was friends with my best friend's mom, and I would see him once or twice a year at the Tebbanowski's house, not really sure why. What I remember is little Johnny—and this dude wasn't even three years old yet, could name every country's flag and describe it in detail. You'd say the country, he'd describe the flag. You'd describe the flag, he'd tell you the country. Blew my mind, this kid. I was maybe eight or so, and I didn't know shit compared to Johnny Veenci.

"Ecuador. A horizontal tricolor of yellow (double width), blue, and red with the National Coat of Arms superimposed at the center. The Coat of Arms features Mount Chimborazo and the steamboat Guayas, drifting on the river of the same name inside an oval topped by a condor."

Yes! That's exactly what Johnny told me. Funny thing was his mother didn't seem impressed. Already an old hat with her by then, I guess.

Years later, I'm talking decades, I was living out in L.A. (Manhattan Beach, to be exact) and the roomies and I were playing Drunk Jeopardy—because that's what we did when we all finally got home from work—and there was this smart guy giving answers on the show and, damn, if it wasn't Johnny Veenci! He still had the brain power I remembered from my youth, but no dexterity whatsoever. Johnny went down in flames that day, another in a long line of Mensa types overwhelmed by the simple demands of the buzzer thingy.

"Here you are señor. Your eggs."

Quito was back, breaking me out of my reverie and returning me to the present moment. He placed before me a sizeable plate of perfectly cooked fried eggs and a tower of toast made from some sweet bread that tasted like brioche, accompanied by delicious guava jelly.

"Aw, Quito, my man. This is perfect."

"Enjoy."

As Quito began his retreat, my curiosity got the better of me.

"Hey, lemme ask you something."

He turned and waited.

"Quito. You named for the capital city? Were you born there, or what's the deal? I'm just curious."

Quito responded by snapping to attention and offering me a salute as he proudly proclaimed his birth name. "Javier Fortunato Edgarto Quishpe at your service."

I was caught off guard, more specifically with a huge mouth of food, so I just pointed at my jaw and nodded.

Quito was content to wait me out.

"That, too, is quite a mouthful," I eventually managed to say. "So, why Quito?"

"There was a rather large man from Houston, one of your oil men. Portly, I believe is the nice way to put it. At the time, my name tag had only my last name, 'Quishpe,' on it, which proved too much for this man as the night went on. By the end of the evening, which was also the end of his second, yes, second bottle of miske, I was 'Quito.' Close enough, yes? I like to be different, and I thought it might help my tour business, so I became Quito."

"That's brilliant. So, what is miske, or do I want to know?" It was a reasonable question, and I was looking for something to occupy him so I could stuff another egg and toast combo into my eager mouth.

"It is made from wild agave, at least ten years old. Very smooth. Very delicious. Very dangerous," Quito cautioned.

"Okay, so it's basically tequila," I managed to say by shoving the last half of toast to one side and trying not to display the remaining contents in my mouth as I shattered one of my mama's few rules and talked with my mouth full.

"If I am a portly Texas oilman!" Quito protested mildly.

"Okay, so maybe not so much like tequila. I'll have to check it out at some point, but not for breakfast."

"That is wise." Quito smiled and was beckoned away, so I took another hit of coffee from his carafe and flashed the okay sign as I wrapped up. I glanced over at the deck railing. It appeared as though I was being stalked by a very weird looking gray bird. Imagine if Grandpa Munster and

Sting both inhabited a finch. Spiky, V-shaped hair with a white streak in the middle. Quito was clearing a nearby table. I motioned him over.

"The fuck is that?" I asked, surprised at the unintentional f-bomb.

I got his super smile in return. "That is a tyrannulet. It will not harm you."

"I don't know...sounds a lot like tyrannosaurus to me."

Quito smiled again. "You finished, señor?"

I backed away from my empty plate. "Nothing left, Quito. Thank you. I believe I'm just going to sit here a bit, take in the view, and see if I can get along with the dinosaur bird."

Quito nodded as he took my plate and scurried away. My surroundings truly were beautiful. A fair number of people were already starting to populate the beach and continue their quest for the perfect tan, but I was content just to think of Maezie and marvel at this place she picked for us, sight unseen. Once more, my stomach began to tighten, in a good way, as I thought of seeing her in the next few days.

I didn't linger over the whys or other specifics of this spur-of-the-moment rendezvous. It was all essentially a blur. I got where I was coming from—fresh from being dumped by my wife of eighteen years who, if I was being honest, was way too young and finally decided to trade me in for a model that was more age appropriate, without the mileage and maintenance issues I was beginning to experience. But I wondered where all this had landed in Maezie's world.

My mind unlocked a long-forgotten memory and left me to connect the dots.

I was maybe six years old and messing with a box of kitchen matches in the woods behind my house in Alexandria, Virginia. My best friend, Mark, and the O'Haro boys were with me, and we thought it a good idea to set ablaze the pile of dried leaves we'd grown weary of jumping into. The cute, little glow quickly exploded into a raging fire, and we ran away frightened, leaving Mother Nature to solve the problem.

Had I lit another careless fire? Would I run from the consequences once more?

"Quito!" I surprised myself with the volume of my summons, and he came immediately to my side. "That miske stuff," I said as a devilish grin spread across my face. "How is it in orange juice?"

3

The Four Before

What was I even doing? It was like I was on some sort of autopilot. I'd cleared my schedule, planned an excursion, hopped a plane—all typical me. Except, now, here I was—in Ecuador. And now, this clearly brainless version of myself was sampling the local hooch, anything to keep from rationalizing and justifying whatever the hell the trip was supposed to be about.

"I can't keep doing this, Kenzie. I'm sorry."

That was what she'd said to me the last time I'd seen Maezie in person. Decades ago. Marriages ago. Children ago. And yet, the very first moment I was able to find a way around the rage of my pending divorce, I'd made it my singular focus to find her once more. I needed Liesel Almay Whoever-the-Hell-She-Was-Now, and I damn sure knew she needed me. What was in bounds and what was out didn't matter in the slightest.

The first sip of miske seared open what used to be my bronchial tubes with a burn I was not expecting. And that's when the familiar debate took hold. It started with a review of my recent sad attempts at dating. Let's just call that collection: The Four Before. Ten seconds in to my first miske and OJ, and I could tell this was going to do the trick. What trick? That was the real question my mind wanted—but refused—to toy with as I took two determined gulps.

"I want to look into Ecuador," Maezie'd told me via text sometime during the first few weeks of our renewed volleys. "The dollar goes so much further there, and the climate is nice. And the beaches are beautiful."

Sold! Was she talking with me about her future or talking about her future with me?

"You really love me, don't you? Unless I'm misinterpreting here..."

Oh, fuck no. You and me. Ecuador. Anywhere.

It was a turn-on that I could reach her like that. I was only a few weeks into the abyss of my separation, reeling, lost, and there came Maezie to the rescue. She'd restore my heart. She would be mine. Correction: She *is*...mine.

Somewhere in the stumblings of my youth, someone lost to time once told me that, perhaps, I fall hard for the women that interest me not because I have some innate ability to detect soul mates on sight, but because I am in love with the idea of being in love. In which case, the needier the partner, the better. This was the homeless shelter my heart found refuge in post-divorce as I debated, yet again, my ability to achieve and sustain the kind of relationship I desperately crave whenever I witness couplehood in its various trappings. The kind of relationship Maezie and I had mastered at a very young age.

Julia Roberts as Vivian Ward in *Pretty Woman* summed it up nicely when Richard Gere's character asked her what she expected from the ultimate relationship. *"I want the fairytale,"* she replied.

No one wants to see me in black, patent-leather thigh-highs, I thought as I flashed back to the movie poster. Was I trying to remake Maezie into something she wasn't and never could be?

• • •

I didn't take the first step toward reentering the dating pool until my divorce from Not Maezie was final. In Louisiana, that meant a whole year of separation, even though we'd both moved on to separate lives in separate residences. The first six months were poison, hissing at each other over every slight fluctuation in the pickup and drop-off schedule of our daughter, and seeking revenge in any form, in any moment, for any level of satisfaction.

Once the official divorce decree had posted, I turned to online dating. It seemed to make sense as a place to begin the natural selection process by weeding out the women that looked like John Goodman in drag and those whose profiles read like one wrong move and they'd be boiling your bunny. I passed on the women who listed all the things they weren't looking for in a partner as their opening salvo. Over a rather short period—that included my joining and cancelling memberships in the top three online dating sites within hours of paying the ante to view my prospects in crisp focus—I'd found a woman who seized my heart. Yes, her photo had been attractive, but it was her profile that kept me transfixed. It was not what she'd had to say, but what she did not that I found so refreshing.

My first paramour lived five hours away in Houston and told me she didn't want a long-distance relationship. Oh, that would never do. I would change her mind. And I did. We had one date, and I got the kiss I was hoping for at the end of it. But she'd found a nice way to say— waiting twenty-five minutes for a way into the conversation I was having about my ex—that my mojo was still under reconstruction. It was a fair point. Next!

It was on that torturous drive back from Houston that I realized the yardstick I was wielding in my return to the dating game did not belong to my ex at all but to my long-absent Maezie. The three that followed Houston would only confirm this as they each fell in succession. Austin. Mobile. Charleston. I'd searched far and wide and had come up short every time.

4

Cara Mia

It's curious how our memories become selective as we age. The thoughts are all stored there somewhere in our subconscious, but the paths to some of them simply are no longer that well defined, or for others are grown over and must be hacked out to bring them back into use.

I am oft times amazed at what I recall, seemingly out of nowhere, and other times hugely disappointed that I can't remember significant chunks of time from my life. But I've discovered that if I focus and take myself back to that time or surround myself with friends or music from that particular era, the paths to those memories reemerge.

In recent months, I'd taken a Japanese hand scythe to the myriad of overgrown trails that had led to Maezie. The more I uncovered, the more I realized just how special, how all-consuming, our love was.

Forty-plus years ago, I met Maezie Fock for the first time, and I recall it like it was yesterday. (To be fair, that particular trail has been carefully maintained all these years.) It was September of 1980, a Friday night, the fifth to be exact....

• • •

The temperature in Shreveport has settled at a very pleasant 72° after having been near 100° during the day, and Centenary College of Louisiana is just underway with the fall semester. I'm starting my third but not necessarily junior year at my mother's alma mater where I'm one of 1,050 students currently enrolled.

Centenary is a real place, "the oldest college west of the Mississippi," founded in 1825. While I will fictionalize many people and places during the course of this tale, my beloved college is not one of them. Great teachers, great scholars, great fun, great memories.

Cara Mia's is a local dive bar and Centenary hangout. You can gain admission if you look anywhere around eighteen or so, the draft beer is cheap, a plate of spaghetti can be had for $1.35, and the joint even has a few pool tables for those whose dating strategy is to simply be awesome at the game as a conversation starter that hopefully leads to a weekend score. I am no pool wizard, so I can be found on the back patio overlooking the scenic yet creepy Greenwood Cemetery, milling about with members of my fraternity during some sort of "meet and greet" the school has unofficially encouraged as if we won't know every last detail of every resident student at our little college soon enough. It's early in the evening, and the sun is just beginning its fade from the sky.

"Mia's," as I alluded to earlier, is unassuming, essentially a one-story, metal building on a wedge of land in the turn where Market Street becomes Centenary Boulevard as it heads south toward the college. The red, white, and green striped structure is a nod to the owner's Italian heritage, the name means "my beloved," and it is here, tonight, where I will learn just how apropos said name for the setting truly is. From this point forward, no longer will I first recall "Cara Mia" as part of the love vocabulary of Gomez Addams, one of the many pet names he had for his beloved Tish. It will forever be the place I first met *my* one and only...*my* beloved.

Oh, I will regale you with every descriptor I can summon when my eyes settle on Maezie for the first time, of that you can be sure. But my introduction to her life force is about to come via a different sensory input here in a moment.

I hear her laugh, and it's the first of a one-two combo delivered to perfection. Looking back, my heart never had a chance.

I'm drawn to laughter. It's my stock-in-trade. Growing up an only child in the Church household, I was subjected to adult conversations early on and soon discovered I could more easily exist in that world if I was funny, so I practiced my humor and tailored it to try and please my father and his friends. It worked to some degree, but even when I fell short of the mark, it taught me to be fearless, and the more I practiced, the better I got. Here and there I scored the belly laugh, and nothing made me prouder than to see a big smile on my father's face and have him praise me in front of his friends. I lived for that, ever chasing my father's elusive approval.

With her light and gentle offering to the night air, a Dolly Parton warble of a laugh, Maezie's mirth has found me. She's speaking my language. I can't tell you who she's with, not that it's somehow forbidden or incriminating knowledge. It's just my focus is instantly drawn to the source, so genuine and heartfelt and, once my eyes lock on her, all secondary occupants become tertiary in the grand scheme of things. I have more than a moment to take in the glorious creature no more than eight feet from me, and she is resplendent. Maezie is poised before a wooden picnic table, one of several that serve as glorified drink holders for the assembled throng. Off to the side is a weathered ArklaGas grill that I'm confident hasn't been used since *The Banana Splits* was a popular Saturday morning show, and behind that, beyond the waist-high, chain-link fence, is the cemetery's wooden shed that we all assume holds whatever tools gravediggers use these days. The proprietor of Mia's has taken it upon himself to paint the one shiplap wall of the shed that faces his property red, and I mean

RED, with yellow trim in what I can only assume is some sort of homage to spaghetti and meat sauce.

What I'm hearing soothes me like the harps of Heaven, invites me in. And what I will quickly learn is that Liesel Almay Fock is laughing at her own joke. For she, much like me—so much like me—has honed the gift of humor to her advantage and is the one holding court at the moment. Her hairstyle is a departure this evening, something I will come to know in the months ahead as she reveals herself to be glorious and inventive—a master of style—even at an annoying T-1 class at 7:50 in the morning where most of us, well, guys anyway, pull on some scrub pants or coveralls and trudge 'cross campus half asleep.

She has her hair cut short, reminiscent of Florence Henderson's look on *The Brady Bunch* toward the end of that show's run, only Maezie's hair is dark brown, and her bangs are straight down, more like Liza Minnelli in *Cabaret*, just touching her amazingly expressive eyes that have been highlighted to radiate well into the night with just the right amount of liner and eye shadow, stopping short of Egyptian but equally as mesmerizing. Her mouth rests open in the most charming position, tongue pushing between the rows of perfectly white teeth as if forming the start of the word "thistle."

This is Forever Maezie, and precisely the moment I fall in love.

She returns my gaze, and we are both smitten. The second punch sends me reeling.

"Oh, hello," she remarks as if discovering an unexpected tadpole under a rock in some quiet brook during one of the glorious fall mornings I envision her delighting in on a regular basis. The space separating us seems to collapse in that instant. Now, normally a guy like me would glance over one shoulder to confirm I'm the one being addressed, but a) I don't want to break eye contact with her lest she vaporize along with the dream I assume I am having, and b) I know in that moment I am her intended, or don't care even if I'm not because I will be before either of us leaves the meager patio of Cara Mia's, of that I have zero doubt.

"Hello yourself," I manage to deliver in the one and only moment in my history on this planet where my response to a woman of interest is both succinct and appropriate. I advance to her and honestly have no idea what becomes of the others in her group. Maybe I'm introduced, maybe they stand by and watch.... I don't know or care.

"I'm Kenzie," I say as I offer my dry hand as my left is busy clutching the sweaty remains of my beer cup. What comes next is, by all outward appearances, a simple and cordial handshake, a greeting witnessed countless times every day by all manner of people. For us, however, the exchange lasts longer than the rules of simple greeting prescribe. It feels as though we've connected with some sort of charging station meant only for us. And for the first time, I feel the air rush from my body.

"I'm Liesel," she says as she swallows, and I note she is in no better shape than I am. "Call me Maezie. Or, I don't know, just whatever."

I'm not the only one nervous here. Good. But now, I'm thoroughly confused, and I need to get this right, so I point to the monogram on her shirt, going over each letter one at a time. "Liesel. Dunno. Maezie." She thinks this is funny or is just being kind. I don't care because the mirthful laugh is back, and her eyes ascend to another level of Heaven.

"Laura Magee," she clarifies, which proves no help. "She was my roomie last year at Kilgore. One too many late-night taco runs, I guess, so she gave me the shirt. Guess I should think about having the monogram removed, huh?"

I smile and nod. "What's the D stand for?"

"I'm not really sure. In view of the fact she was my friend and that she just gave me this expensive shirt without even trying to get the pounds off...maybe 'Dumbass'?"

Oh, the laughter comes easy in this moment. I'm in paradise, stranded on an island with the beautiful, charming, and funny Maezie Something. This is unbelievable.

We stand there, we talk, we absorb one another. I get us more beers, even though neither of us are much on drinking them. We no longer need the courage found in that foam.

"Kilgore," I continue. "Were you a Rangerette?" Visions of the renowned Texas answer to the even more renowned Radio City Rockettes fill my mind only briefly as Maezie sets me straight.

"No, I was in the orchestra. Violin."

"Do you still play?" Maezie studies me to make sure I'm serious, which I am.

"I do."

"That's spectacular. Maybe you could play something for me sometime. Brahms. Sibelius. Mendelssohn. Your pick." I'm still being studied, then smiled at with what I can see is pure joy in Maezie's eyes.

"I'd like that. But only if you take me to a movie first."

"Done!" I blurt out before the butterflies in my stomach can lodge in my throat, and then there follows the most amazing and satisfying silence either of us has ever experienced.

A pact has been made, an historic charter of some sort, and we must allow the ink to dry lest we smudge something and mar the moment. Maezie and I memorize each other, in no hurry whatsoever, feeling no need to keep up the conversation. There is no awkwardness to be found in our little world. We both know in this instant all the greatness and wonder of that world is ours to discover. Let the magic begin!

Inspired by Gomez Addams and not in the least by the metal building at my back, I utter the first thing that comes to mind as I step forward and take Maezie's hands in mine, and we both flinch ever so slightly when we feel the energy pass between us again. I'm transfixed by her radiant beauty and become hopelessly lost in her eyes. Slowly, we find our rhythm of breathing coming back into line, and in sync with one another as words finally surface, encouraged by her unyielding gaze. "Cara Mia."

So perfect is this moment. There's nothing left to want for either of us save the total submission to one another.

The kiss, the heart-melding seal of the deal defies description even to this day.

"You and me. Why not?!" she asks with eager eyes.

Indeed.

・・・

If you ever asked me to paint a portrait of her from that evening, I could capture her likeness and have earned my living from such at various points in time.

She was wearing jeans that fit her to perfection, the indigo so dark and crisp upon them, they had to be new. Topping the ensemble was a yellow, long-sleeved oxford with a button-down collar. The preppy look was just coming back into fashion, and Maezie was ahead of the curve, as always. Her shoes were a dark-navy moccasin, I think. But, truthfully, my eyes never dipped below her waist that evening. On the pocket of her shirt was *LDM* in a navy Hampton Diamond font, which, of course, was where our conversation began.

I must've been smiling like a total dork when I waved my empty glass in Quito's direction. He accommodated me with another miske and OJ.

I was lost in the past and liking it.

5

Jaycee

John Charles. I don't think actually knew he was gay when we were in college, or if he did, he didn't vocalize it, not to imply he didn't broadcast it in other ways because the boy was delightfully flamboyant and a reliable source of entertainment for Maezie and me during the formative months of our relationship.

Formative? Who am I kidding?

Our relationship was fully formed from the get-go, I just wouldn't be in any big hurry to go bandying about the word "mature" in the same sentence, for we both had a ways to go in that department. *And maybe there's still some modicum of work to be done there.*

"Jaycee" as we came to call the occupant of the front, right dorm room in my primo suite on the ground floor of Pierce Cline dormitory, came from money, but enough about that. Jaycee had the most amazing orange hair that always had the appearance of being blown by unseen winds. Aggressive winds. Picture Bozo and you wouldn't be too far off the mark. He drove a tricked-out 442 Hurst Olds, maroon over white with rotating front bucket seats. And when I say he "drove" it, I mean, a lot. That car was his therapy in the most literal sense of the word.

And Jaycee had a laugh that was instantly identifiable. It was loud, actually terrifying, and would often come without warning. But it was also genuine and infectious. And Jaycee had another "signature" quality, if you will, a mannerism I can only describe as a time delay of some sort whereby he cogitated on things until he felt he understood them, and this often affected his ability to answer you within any sort of reasonable time frame, which left you wondering if the boy was in the midst of some sort of seizure.

Wearing his emotions on his sleeve and everywhere else, it was hard to say what might upset my suite mate as his world was very fluid. But when he got heated, he'd have that sort of bull terrier about-to-be-hit-in-the-forehead-with-a-sledgehammer look. Then, within seconds of that, Jaycee would feel for his car keys and march toward the nearest exit with a "I just have to drive!"

And we wouldn't see the guy for hours, at least, maybe days.

Now, this was decades before Amazon took over home delivery of every blessed want or need, but I tell you, Jaycee was dialed in to some catalog company back then because he was forever taking delivery of all manner of boxes filled with gadgetry, clothing, food, and whatever wants he needed sating. The first time I ever saw a pair of hundred-dollar sunglasses was atop Jaycee's orange mop, perched like a headband and holding on for dear life to the flaming nest the color of a desert sunset.

"Serengetis," he intoned with pride, as if I knew anything about sunglasses beyond Foster Grant.

I nodded mostly to myself at having come close with the desert sunset analogy for his hair.

Every Sunday night at eight was the weekly meeting of my fraternity. Let's just call them the Delta boys in honor of *Animal House*. We'd gather at the start of the new week to discuss the pressing business of our organization—how many kegs we could afford for an upcoming blowout, what new and creative ways we could figure out how to approach the alumni about that fireplace we wanted to add to the chapter house, who would play Santa this year at the annual Christmas visit to the Shriner's Hospital for Children (we could be useful!), etc. And then, the end of the meeting was reserved for an informal gossip session known as FGO, which stood for "For the Good of the Order." Although I never fully understood how salacious gossip about sorority girls or the latest deviltry perpetrated against the Dean of Students benefitted the chapter, but it was always a grand time and a perfect stage for me.

On one particular Sunday, Jaycee failed to show. By some miracle he'd been elevated from a lowly pledge to active status the previous semester. Truly, I think the guys enjoyed his unpredictable nature and flamboyance as much as I did, or they thought his old man a proper target of future fundraising efforts. ("Pledge 'em and drain 'em" was a saying we employed on occasion, not always in jest.)

There was little in the way of formal business to attend to, so we were just easing into FGO when the front door of the chapter house flew open and in popped Jaycee dressed in a matching red-over-white Sergio Tacchini tennis outfit that was glowing and glorious against his pale and freckled Nordic skin. Riding the mop were the Serengetis. Jaycee scared the shit out of us with his entrance because, as a general rule, the front door was supposed to be locked during the meeting. But someone (and the list of backup someones) had forgotten to check that detail after the litany of ins and outs at the start of our gathering. Several people surged toward the door, ready to defend the house from rival frats, I suppose, and another one or two went to obscure the treasured paraphernalia that was used in the ritualistic ceremonies of our order lest it be compromised by outside eyes.

Much like Cosmo Kramer, Jaycee knew how to make an entrance, and he'd outdone himself in that moment. He held his head high and announced to our assemblage, "I have arrived."

This statement of the obvious was met with a combination of groans and head shaking as the brethren relaxed from attack stance and returned to their seats amid grumblings that included the word "fuck." The chapter vice president, who was also in charge of fining any member he felt violated procedure or proper protocol, had his own obvious declaration.

"You're late! I'm fining you the sum of one dollar."

Jaycee's response was one that would live in infamy. A student of the credit card (dorm deliveries on top of dorm deliveries), he rarely, if ever, carried cash on his person.

"Where am *I* gonna get a dollar?"

Uproarious laughter ensued.

"Not my problem, Jaycee," our procurator continued. "Pay up or carry your ass."

Uh-oh. This last remark triggered a stall out, and the bull terrier made an appearance, looking around the room at the assembled brotherhood, perhaps for help.

"I'll pay the damn thing," I said from my perch at the officer's table.

I'd recently been elected chapter Scribe and was in charge of note-taking at meetings, whatever correspondence we had with the national organization, and the all-important duty of sharing our accomplishments in the weekly Greek Beat of the school newspaper, which I'd perverted into a total lampoon column.

"I'll just come back another time," Jaycee offered with all the presence of a neighbor lady who'd come calling at the dinner hour.

And with that, he stepped for the door but was met with shouts of "Back door!" as a reminder of the proper egress during the meeting.

Jaycee acknowledged the commands of his brethren and was soon heard exiting the kitchen.

• • •

I truly had the best dorm room in all of Centenary, not for the décor, even though I'd done wonders with my assigned space in the days before Command strips or their future spokesman, M.C. Hammer, was there to help hang things on cinder block walls. No, my room was ideally situated on the ground floor, on the side opposite the main entrance, away from the prying eyes of the resident assistants and resident director. Centenary had no co-ed dorms and there was a curfew that had to be observed, at least in theory. Maezie and I tested that theory on more than one occasion.

As sharp in my memory as the night of our first meeting, this second pathway back to the fall of 1980 was every bit as well worn.

The curfew was midnight. All members of the opposite sex had to be gone from the living quarters—although I believe it was still okay to hang in the lobby "studying." Maezie and I found it easy to sit and talk for hours, and did so as often as humanly possible, which was often since we'd begun flagrantly ignoring our studies in the earliest days of our relationship. We'd settle in the Student Union Building, the cafeteria, the library, and outdoor spaces, or take inspiration from Jaycee and grab my car and "just drive." There was a hunger to know one another, to affirm we had the same likes and dislikes, borne of similar experiences. As we grew in comfort, we grew in intimacy.

One night, not long into the seemingly vertical trajectory of our romance, Maezie and I conspired to game the system. At the appointed hour of midnight, I walked her out to and through the lobby, being sure we both said goodnight to Stan the Resident Director. He was a nice enough guy. Maezie had helped that relationship along by flashing him her gorgeous smile and offering Stan several sentences more in small talk than most any other person on campus ever did, so it wasn't surprising to see him smile and return her parting wave as she very publicly made her departure from Cline, pairing off with another single girl headed back to their side of campus. I stood there and watched and waved, genuinely missing what had so quickly become "my other half."

Reluctantly, I sauntered back through the lobby, stopping for a moment to make my own small talk with Stan and a girl named Graham, who never seemed to leave the table in the corner. I accepted her offer of a handful of popcorn with appropriate thanks, bid them good night, and returned to my dorm room where I went to my ground floor window, raised the thick, heavy, metal blinds, opened the portal, and reached my hand out to help my beloved Maezie over the sill and back to where she belonged.

We coupled, and paradise was defined anew.

One o'clock found us happily spooned together, purring like kittens and out cold. To this day, when I see a stack of spoons in the kitchen drawer, it takes me back. If we needed further proof we were made for one another, that was it, at least until the blaring sound shocked us awake, and we flew into panic mode. No, Jaycee had not released one of his famous guffaws in the room next door. Far worse. The fire alarm was sounding, and we had to act fast.

I was little help to Maezie as I had only recently figured out the mystery of unhooking a bra and was clueless about how to reverse the process, so I pulled on my jeans, which caught on my thighs and sent me tumbling first into the mattress then onto the floor. *Make that Maezie's jeans.* The "D" for "Dumbass" belonged solely to me that night. She laughed, then I laughed before donning my T-1 uniform of scrub pants and helping her with her sweater.

The hurried moments then came to a screeching halt when it came time to say "goodnight" for real. Maezie and I had no room to criticize Jaycee and his near-coma stall-outs because we were guilty of the same in simply trying to find the words to express our love and admiration for one another.

We had only seconds to spare when Maezie had the wisdom to end our kiss with a gentle push back and the sweetest little half wave as she climbed out the window into the night.

Getting caught with a member of the opposite sex in your dorm room at Centenary would not only result in a write-up, but pretty much guarantee an appearance before the tribunal that administered the Methodist-based university, a shaming where one would be reminded that "liberal" did not apply to conjugal arts education.

But those damn ancient, metal blinds made one hell of a noise as the pull cord disappeared with her. I ran to the sill and looked down. There, sprawled on the ground like all the dirty laundry in my cramped closet was precious Maezie, done in by the blind cord and the outside drop-off that was a few feet lower than the inside.

"Are you okay?" I asked her, trying to contain my freakout while the door to the suite next to mine slammed open. I will never, ever, *ever*, forget the look on Maezie's face as she found her feet once more, dusted off her wounded palms, and met my gaze.

"Can I come back?"

Freeze on that moment.

I was a young man of twenty who'd just fallen totally and helplessly in love with what I believed was the one person I was destined to be with. I had never known this sentiment before, never seen it by example from my parents or anyone else in my two decades on Earth, and somewhere in my dysfunctional mind, I didn't think I was worthy of such love. Yet, the look I received in that moment said otherwise. I wanted to believe, I really did. The scene was allowed to progress, and her words came at me in stunning crystal boxes, beautiful treasures for any man but quite simply unfathomable to me even as I heard them.

"Woo-hoo!" or whatever the hell I offered in response was delivered in toto before I released the cord and those awful and heavy blinds—nothing "mini" about them—crashed onto the sill, obscuring the window at the exact moment Stan flung open my door and screamed at me to join every other soul in the yard for assembly and head-count.

"Yes, of course!" I responded, not to Stan but as a postscript to my Maezie who was still within earshot.

...And return, she did. Oh, glory.

Stan learned of this some months later. We were so well known on campus as an item by then, that there was no point in trying to pull a fast one on anybody.

By the fourth drill, the dutiful resident director greeted us with a matter-of-fact "hey, guys" when Maezie and I strolled from F Suite in our matching technicolor robes to join the rest of Cline in the yard for the head count. Our garb became the immediate envy of Jaycee, who wasted no time cozying up to us for a better look.

By the fifth fire drill, Jaycee had a dorm-delivered technicolor robe all for himself.

We made quite the trio and looked way ahead of our time in that lineup. His arm wasn't hooked in, but it might as well have been.

6
The Fourth's Estate

My mother, Loraine, was born a Fleming, not so much a noteworthy name in the states but a treasured one in Scotland from whence her people originated. She and, therefore, I descend from Lady Jane Fleming, granddaughter of King James IV and on, back into history.

The Flemings arrived in Shreveport rather abruptly in 1888. My great-grandfather, Homer, had a men's clothing store in Arcadia, some fifty miles or so east, but had become smitten with a young woman and decided he must move his entire operation to Shreveport to be near to her and woo her with all due haste. Julia was a feisty young thing, much like my Maezie, and I could easily see how my romantic sensibilities came forth from Homer as the letters of his that survived in his mammoth scrapbook—which have served to chronicle the entire Fleming history in

America—put my efforts to shame. Homer was a wordsmith of the highest order, and that guy was consumed by his love for Julia. Sound familiar?

After a reasonable courtship of a year and a half, Homer and Julia were married in the fall of 1890, and the haberdashery became firmly rooted in the community. The store was inherited by their three children upon Homer's passing in 1948, and his son Joe, the lone male, eventually bought out his sisters and settled into the perfect job that allowed him to indulge in his passion for fishing as much as he desired. Fleming & Burns continued its reign into my lifetime as essentially a men's social club, where just enough clothing transactions took place each day to legitimize the operation financially and appease the wives of the well-dressed patrons of Shreveport.

As the only child of Joe and his bride, Mamie, my mother Loraine, stood to inherit the family enterprise at some point in time. That point arrived prematurely during our vacation to Louisiana in the summer of 1970, when rat-chewed wires ignited a fire in the attic of the Fleming home that claimed the lives of her parents and my only sibling, my older sister, Amy.

Shreveport reeled from this news as my thoroughly broken parents struggled to make sense of the tragedy and find a way forward.

I was shuttled among the relatives while every emotion from unknowable sadness to outright rage tested the fabric of their union until irreparable damage was done. Then came the triple funeral followed by some sort of retreat to

Florida for ten days of I-don't-know-what before returning to Virginia.

Must've been to figure out: What next?

My dad was over Alexandria and all the Beltway politics. My mother confessed she had no desire to return to the city of her birth—that she was happy in Alexandria as a member of the Marlan Forest Garden Club. But my father saw tremendous opportunity in my mother's family's business, Fleming & Burns, and somebody had to run it. So, Judd ultimately prevailed, and Shreveport became our home once more the following year.

I remember thinking the new home was huge. The neighborhood, known as Pepper Ridge, consisted of about fifty homes centered around a small lake. It was five miles south of town and afforded the feel of country living on evenly spaced lots of an acre or more. Shortly after unpacking my three suitcases and gazing out my new bedroom window at who knows what, I watched as two kids around my age strolled across my new lawn and up to my door on the afternoon of July first, toting a couple of .22 rifles. It was Scoon Penn and Mike Nabe, and they'd become part of my new gang of friends and make life as a now only child more manageable.

I showed them my room and was invited along on their afternoon adventure. I didn't have a gun but went with them anyway to witness their efforts at abating the snake population on Bayou Pierre. Within weeks, I had my own .22, and a Honda 50 minibike like theirs was added to my Christmas wish list.

• • •

My father had a background in a lot of things, advertising being but one of his talents, so for his next feat, he set about growing and transforming Fleming & Burns through a dedicated ad campaign and expansion of the operation to the 6,000-square-foot third floor of the store's post-war location that hadn't been used for anything but storage since the days when it was among the largest retailers of Levi's in America.

Overnight, the once tiny Arcadia enterprise became known as "The largest men's store in the entire southwest!" as my father proudly proclaimed on his Sunday night commercials that aired right before the sports report on the late news.

Former congressional politico, Mackenzie Judson Rowe Church III was now "Judd" Church, the friendly and impeccably dressed pitch guy, posed on a lone stool before a plant and a dark screen, giving his version of a fireside chat that people actually paid attention to for a change. He became somewhat of a celebrity, among the downtown crowd anyway, and was soon serving on a number of boards of directors and the Downtown Development Authority.

I was with him once, years later, after he'd traded his extracurricular community endeavors to be the producer and host of the world-famous Louisiana Hayride radio and stage show. We were making our way back from lunch, when a man approached him with a puzzled look, waving his finger and inserting himself in our way. "Didn't you used to be Judd Church?" the man inquired, obviously missing those reliable Sunday night commercials now gone from the newscast.

Without missing a beat, my father said, "Yes. Yes, I did."

• • •

My first job at Fleming & Burns was sorting boxes of coat hangers on the third floor when it was being prepped to become the new home to more than a thousand suits. I was eleven and glad for the job that would provide me some spending money, even if it meant giving up the occasional Saturday to earn it. That job complete, I was promoted to elevator operator for the small Otis lift, circa 1947, and took great pride in factoring in the coasting distance of the box once you let off the lever so that the thresholds would line up perfectly when I pulled back on the bar to allow my passengers egress. I recall a small access panel in the wall of the elevator shaft, in between the mezzanine and the third floor, where I took delight in staging mannequin hands or rubber rats on its ledge to surprise the construction workers or store employees as we rode the open front lift to the top floor. Soon, I would know every nook and cranny of that 20,000+ square foot building.

Don Mangam was one of our top suit salesmen and, also, one heck of an artist. He eventually took me under his wing and began grooming me as the replacement for his other job of window dresser, and I said goodbye to the entertaining elevator operator gig.

Don taught me how to set type for the signs in the window, how to hand paint the flowing cursive titles, how to properly pin a suit, and how to stage an effective and eye-catching display. By fifteen, I was in charge of all displays for what had become the largest men's store in the South. Little did I know, the skills Don so patiently taught me would surface decades later when I became a set dresser in the movies.

Throughout high school and on into college, I worked at the store at least on the weekends. Once we opened a second location in a local mall, I began working some nights as well. My father was pleased with my diligence and was anxious for me to take the reins of the business so he could stop worrying about it and focus full time on finding the next big star on his precious Hayride. Seeing my father chase his passion only made me want to do the same, but he had other plans for me. "Do as I say and not as I do" became his indefensible mantra that I was expected to swallow whole when he traded his three-piece suits for sequins during the summer of 1974.

The day I was born, my horoscope advocated that the creative child born that day would have oodles of friends because of the rare magnetism in my chart. I should be given the best education possible, it cautioned, and instilled with a strong work ethic or...*the latter years become difficult.* When my teen years arrived in the rearview mirror,

I found myself fighting those creative Gemini impulses on a daily basis and began to realize that *the latter years* were now upon me.

7

Every Time I Think of You

I've got to at least try to do this. I have to attempt to quantify what I was feeling as I came to know Maezie Fock, or you'll never truly grasp the point of this whole missive.

It's not a difficult thing for Yours Truly to speak from the heart on the topic of love, as you well know, dear reader. But to do so in a way as to ensure others stay tuned—well, therein lies the challenge. This is why I've subtitled this volume, *A Vital Novel*. I have this energy that must be released back into the universe, perhaps so another can come to be addicted as I am to the greatest gift of all.

Music has always been a tool of expression for me. My experiences handling musical instruments have consisted of a foray with a trumpet in fifth grade band (coronet, actually), and what I will call "a brief encounter" with the banjo during my high school years, unless you want to count playing "Twinkle, Twinkle Little Star," parts of "Heart & Soul," and whatever western-sounding song results when you roll your fist across the piano keys as some sort of accreditation to the ever-present Steinway in our home. I have also owned a recording studio, but we'll get to that later, perhaps. No, what I'm talking about here is music as a tool for expressing my heart—through poignant lyrics, a certain cadence in the rhythm, and due to its indelible attachment to a specific moment in time.

• • •

Maezie and I just had to drive one day, and we had the radio on in my smoke-gray Buick Riviera. The sunroof was open, and it was a pleasant early evening as we drove the parkway to nowhere in particular. The armrests were up in the car so Maezie could get right up against me, and I loved how she felt that close in, with the softness of her hair touching my shoulder. Both hands on the wheel was not an option when she and I traveled together. I always had my arm around her. She was unquestionably mine, and I was damn proud of that fact.

I recognized the song playing low in the background and asked Maezie to turn it up, my free hand being otherwise occupied tending her waist. Our love for each other could be overwhelming at times, and this was about to be one such moment. Though I didn't see it coming when I began to softly relay the song lyrics to my other half, and the talk of our never-ending love and our plans to defy the test of time with our grand love affair just landed so very near and dear to my heart.

Although it was not my finest moment as a singer, that ad lib earned me the softest kiss upon my cheek, which sent chills throughout my entire body. I took one last look at the deserted parkway before meeting her lips with mine, ever so briefly, or until the sound of the rumble strips called me back to driving duty. By now the song had worked its way to the chorus, and I spent my pent-up energy on serenading my sweetheart with everything filling my heart.

"I love you so much," Maezie said so thoughtfully at the conclusion of The Babys hit song from the previous year. I felt like a king.

"Even after that pitiful rendition?"

"Mackenzie Church," she scolded, "Especially after that. You sang from your heart, and I know it's real for you, that you mean it...and that makes me feel safe. I mean, look at you! You're crying, for heaven's sake."

"Oh, shit, I am." I checked myself in the rearview mirror. It was true. "Well, the song didn't say anything about *me* not crying."

I'll say it here and now, dear reader. It doesn't have to be a remarkable song. This was a minor hit from a British band that disappeared from the charts altogether very soon after, but it afforded me just the right words at just the right moment, underscoring my tremendous feelings for the woman I held so dear and giving me a way to honor her in that fleeting instant.

Now, decades later, when "Every Time I Think of You" comes on the car radio, I crank it, knowing I'll need to raid my stash of fast-food napkins in the center console before song's end.

Maezie Fock took my appreciation of music to a whole other level. We had many spirited and engaging conversations on the subject of the chart climbers, routinely taking apart some of the songs that didn't belong on Top Forty radio no matter what Dick Clark's followers or Casey Kasem's weekly countdown endorsed.

On one of our Sunday drives to nowhere, the conversation somehow shifted from the slow fade of instrumental songs to the pros and cons of the disco era when Maezie suddenly cut me off mid-sentence.

"Take me to my car. Now!"

"Aw, c'mon," I protested. "You're seriously gonna let the BeeGees come between us?"

She laughed in my face. "You'll never be rid of me that easily, my darling. I just wanna grab a cassette for us to listen to while you drive us somewhere for dinner. Anywhere but Floyd's Barbecue. I swear he used to have a big pack of dogs running around the yard and now there's just two."

"One has three legs," I noted.

"Okay, fine. One and three quarters."

The mirthful laughter. The gorgeous smile. And she called me "darling." God, how I loved it when she called me that. It was so...possessive.

We arrived at the parking lot of Hardin dorm. Maezie vaulted from the Riviera and scurried to her car.

"Got to be one of the Top Five bodies on campus." Scoon Penn, one of my buddies from the wonder years, had moseyed up to the car to watch Maezie run off too. Apparently.

He was right, of course, and I allowed him this one observation but made sure he was well aware Maezie was M-I-N-E, which he already was.

"You done good, Hoss," he said with a nod. "I'm off in search of the other four. Wish me luck."

Scoon and I went back decades—to back-porch philosophy sessions on his parents' ranch, and we were frat brothers as well. Some of the guys called him "Pennball," which was a little too grade school for me, but I called him "Scoon," which I'd adapted from his father's nickname of unknown origin. We'll get to him in a little while.

Maezie returned with a smile and a cassette tape firmly in hand. She scooted to the middle, secured her seat belt, and extracted the tape.

"Whatcha got?"

She showed me the cover as she popped the tape into the player.

"*Hooked on Classics*. You're gonna love it."

And I did. It was all the greatest hits of classical music linked together and set to a modern drumbeat. We drove around the rest of the night listening to and commenting on the various arrangements, stopping briefly at Cobb's Barbecue for chopped beef sandwiches to-go, after assessing the property for dogs or other suspect animals.

Maezie was pleased I shared her love for the classics. Truthfully, I was swayed by her passion for it. She'd close her eyes to better feel the rhythms and invite me to do the same, but I always cheated, preferring to watch her interpret each composition. She knew I was watching and would look at me during key parts, pointing out the introduction of the strings or the unexpected *bomp, bomp, bomp* of a tuba. Because of her, I came to know the bassoon as far more than the mysterious instrument used to make creeping-up sounds as Elmer Fudd closed in on *"...that wascally wabbit."*

Maezie and Kenzie didn't have an "Our Song." We found joy and happiness in so many.

Our enjoyment of music went hand in hand with our enjoyment of each other. What that has come to mean to me is there are now any number of songs that come on classic hits radio and I am back in that Riviera with Maezie jammed up against me. I can smell her hair (Herbal Essence), and my arm is threatening to go dead because I haven't moved it from her waist in over an hour, and we're just driving along, and she's calling me "darling," and the world is perfect.

Recently, I'd searched the track "Hooked on Romance" on my phone and played it on the way home from a much-needed workout in anticipation of our reunion in Ecuador. My favorite selection of the *Hooked on Classics* album, I found the song almost too beautiful as it so clearly summed up the elegance of what Maezie and I had in our college years. The tears fell like rain, as there were no napkins left in the console to mop them up. Even though I would see her once more in a matter of days, I was grieving all those years in the interim, whereby Maezie and I had lost our way from one another and busied ourselves with well-meaning substitutes—who gave us children and tried to love us the best they could—not knowing we measured them with a preconceived yardstick that grazed the stars. The song ended as I turned in my driveway, and I immediately emailed Maezie.

Oh, my Maezie, what I wouldn't give to have those in-between years back. I look through your letters, and I think them the most beautiful words anybody has ever scribed, such a testament of someone completely lost in love, and, somehow, I walked away from that, and a few short months later, you were gone from school and my life.

So, I grieved the past today, caught off guard by its attack. I had to write you to share my grief. And to tell you that I am still looking for that new word for "love," as it needs to go here. I freely add "honor," for I can now properly honor all that you have been and are to me...and, of course, "cherish." Always. Ever. Cherish.

Soon, my beautiful angel. I can't wait...

8

Miske Mania

"Quito! You weren't lying. This—" A mother and her young boy walked into my line of sight, and I cut myself off from what was shaping up to be a drunken rant. I put a finger to my lips and shushed myself, grinning in delight at the orbit my recently overworked consciousness was now entering. Quito came to my side, and I quietly continued.

"This shit is wicked. I've had, what? Two miskes and OJs...?"

Quito pointed at my empty glass. "That was number three."

"Well, they're little, tiny-ass glasses, so really not even two," I justified. "Point is, it's breakfast and I'm fried. I need a friggin' nap. I mean, you tried to warn me, Quito, my man. Yep, always lookin' out for your buddy, Kenzie. I like you, Quito. You're all right."

Quito nodded, and his generous smile was back like the sun from behind the clouds.

"You're gonna love my Maezie, Quito," I raved. "Just not as much as I do, because that's simply not possible. Not like some quantum thing, not that any of us understand that shit. Am I right? Schrodinger's cat. Let the damn thing out of the box already. Anyway, it's just that...well, it's just not possible. I love her so damn much, Quito. You'll see."

"Yes, señor. I will put the charges to your room and perhaps you can have that nap."

"But," I continued, overrunning Quito's sage advice, driven by the need to complete my thought while I still had one. "But we'll go on your coffee tour because Maezie loves a good cup of coffee. Did you know she made Husband Number 3 buy her a damn Jura machine? Do you even know what a Jura machine is? I told Maezie the only Jura I ever heard of was that mountain range in Switzerland, and she thought that was brilliant and wanted to be sure and be my trivia partner on our next trivia thingy. I can't friggin' wait. Hey, you ever play Drunk Jeopardy? Don't answer that. I'm putting myself to bed. You working lunch today, Quito?"

"I am, yes."

"Then I'll try really hard to see you then. Thanks for trying to warn me."

I took my chair with me a foot or more before finally escaping its clutches.

"You're the best," I trailed off as I bounced toward room five.

One thing I had to say for miske was it didn't give me a hangover.

I did, however, wake and immediately commence the search for the cat that took a shit in my mouth. Pretty noxious "morning after" breath—but on the positive side, at least the "morning after" was still today. Well, early afternoon after.

I waved at Quito on my way to the beach to let the sun finish off my purge.

He pointed at his watch and gave a thumbs-up and a flash of the smile I'd come to rely on.

Good guy.

Murcielago Beach was not crowded at that hour, at least not by my standards, which I have to admit are fairly high due to my recent purchase of a condo in Destin, Florida, where the sand was as white as sugar and the water a crisp turquoise. Here the sand was on the brown side of tan but at least it wasn't littered with clumps of seaweed like Galveston.

I found my way to the edge of the rentals, paid the reasonable $5 fee for the day, and plopped down among my three chairs and cabana. Tanning was not something I actively pursued. I was pale enough in college to have earned the nickname "White Boy" or "WB" for short. This was about re-upping my vitamin D and an attempt to finish at least one of the books Maezie told me to read, not that we'd have a shortage of things to talk about when I saw her.

I'd picked up *A Gentleman in Moscow* and was 70 percent through it. It has taken me on a delightful journey thus far. Set in the first half of the twentieth century, and mostly in Moscow—where Count Rostov has been placed under house arrest for having authored a poem that the new Communist regime viewed as inappropriate and inciteful—he's been confined to his residence, which happened to be the glamourous Hotel Metropole. The story revolves around how he managed to live out decades without going stir crazy.

I knew Maezie's attraction to, and subsequent recommendation of, the novel stemmed from the author Amor Towles creating such a proper and refined gentleman as Count Rostov. It was something I have always aspired to be and had maybe even achieved with Maezie.

Okay, fine, you caught me. Bonus points for trying?

There's been more than one incident where she and I encountered one another with purpose during one or more of her marriages. I truly never wanted to be "that guy" nor did Maezie want to be "the other woman" for the simple fact that if we betrayed our vows in a moment of passion or abandoned them for one another, then we would brand ourselves as capable of such and that would surely pose a threat to our bond at some point down the road.

I mean, how do you conspire with a paramour to kill their spouse with only the assurance of "baby, with you and me it's different" to keep you safe in your future escapades? If you've each done it even once, then you're fully capable of it. After that, you're just assessing the odds, which have been running well above 50 percent for a very long time.

We never shattered the vows for that reason, though we had put a couple of hairline cracks in the handblown glass on which those legal contracts were scribed.

But that's the chief reason it's taken forty-plus years to arrive at this moment. And then, of course, pure goddamn timing stepped in to play the crucial role.

I'd made mistakes, she'd made mistakes, and it'd taken that long to separate the goodness of our children and gratitude of invaluable lessons learned from the chaff we allowed ourselves to suffer, and factor in the occasional contribution of maturity, before circling back for one another. I can tell you one thing from this vantage point achieved through deprivation and self-denial, I cherish Maezie all the more and am convinced we'll be together this time around "'til death us *not* part" because we're headed straight for eternity, hand in hand.

I wanted to drink to that sentiment but found my morning miske mania had suitably checked that item off today's list, and well into the foreseeable future. Jaycee would've been proud of the Serengetis I sported as I cracked open my book. The sun felt nice, and I was content.

9
Fleming & Burns

I remember well the summer of 1979. I had only started Centenary College a few weeks earlier, a sort of trial because the grades I was transferring in on—from LSU-Shreveport—were not so hot. My longtime buddy Scoon had sold me on the new college as "a place to hide out within your hometown," surfacing only on the occasional weekend to do laundry at the parents' house.

At nineteen, having been doing the college thing from my grade school bedroom, I was ready for my own place and looked forward to dorm life in the fall.

A job came open in the shoe department that summer, and I steered Scoon toward it. He was an affable salesman and impressed our department head, Larry, from the start. Now, I had a fellow conspirator close at hand, someone to go to lunch and pal around with as we wiled away the time between aging customers on slow Saturdays. The young folks, for the most part, were enjoying the arcades, movie theaters, and indoor comforts of the new "mall" phenomenon and going downtown to shop was seen as more of an anathema than an adventure.

Scoon and I took great delight in analyzing each new customer and making up wild rationalizations as to why they were there with us that day. We were pranksters, well known to the tailor shop and office employees, unafraid to climb into and ride the dumbwaiter to their floor to surprise them when they opened its doors to extract the next suit headed for tailoring.

This particular Saturday, as Scoon and I leaned on the rails of the stairway up to the shoe department on the mezzanine or down to the young men's department in the basement where I worked, an unfamiliar figure came through the front door. It was probably time we got busy anyway, so I drifted forward to see if the man needed any help. Normally, I'd simply retreat to the basement and await the next customer, but I was covering for Margie, the furnishings sales lady, who was at lunch.

"Good afternoon," I greeted the man.

His somewhat beady and rather expectant eyes assessed me like some sort of searchlight. "Can I help you with anything?"

"Naw. Just lookin'," he came back. "I'll holler if I need you."

I glanced at Scoon, several steps above me on the landing, and he made a slow jack-off motion with his hand as he grinned and returned to the shoe department.

I laughed, and the searchlight eyes were back on me. I swallowed my smile and half waved as the man found his way to another department, glad to be rid of me, I'm sure.

Mr. Moreno was the store's master tailor, and I'd spent a few months under his tutelage, learning how to operate a steam press, cuff a pair of pants, and most importantly, how to pin and mark a suit for tailoring. There was an art to it, and I was good at art, so I was soon competent enough to be trusted with fitting customers when Mr. Moreno was too busy with his work or off on his lunch break.

I was in the basement, seated at the sales counter scanning the city's weekly entertainment guide, when I detected someone descending the stairs from above. Seconds later, the searchlight of my earlier customer found me once more. He wanted help selecting a tie to go with his new suit since the ones upstairs were just too "old man looking" for his tastes.

"Got plenty of white shirts at home. Guess blue would work, too, but I could use another tie," he offered as he plopped down his suit on the counter in front of the shirts. I pulled out a wrapped white shirt and slid it under the lapel of his gray-and-blue, chalk-stripe suit, and we went to work. Utilizing part of my training learned under Don Mangam, I could whip a tie around my fingers and create a convincing knot in a matter of seconds, so I sprang into action.

My customer seemed genuinely impressed.

"Are you looking for more of a traditional stripe?" I said as I tucked the first striped tie under the shirt collar and stepped back."

"Hmmm."

I moved on with my pitch. "Or perhaps something more adventurous," I continued, tossing a foulard pattern with gray, blue, and an unusual sherbet highlight into the mix.

"That's interesting."

In an attempt to focus the man where I wanted him, I threw in a decoy. "You're not a paisley sort of guy, are you?" The crazy patterned tie was a great color combo, but I didn't figure it would sit well with this country kind of fellow.

"Aw, hell, no!"

Got a smile out of him, and another one when I summarily dismissed the selection with a backhand that sent it unceremoniously to the floor somewhere behind the counter.

"Oh, here we go," I said, finally pulling out the tie I'd known from the start he would respond to, a nice poly/silk navy-and-maroon blend with a small repeated gray pinstripe.

"Yeah. Now we're talking," he said, and the selection process was concluded. "Can you fit me down here?"

"Yes, I can. Dressing rooms are right over there."

My customer took his suit and made for an open curtain.

I grabbed my white marking chalk and a pin cushion wristband and stood by the triple mirrors, awaiting his return.

The suit fit surprisingly well off the rack, needing only a pinch at the waist and the unhemmed pants marked near 34 inches. I also took half an inch off the jacket cuffs to allow a hint of shirt to show through. Moments later, we were done.

"We should have the suit ready next Saturday, unless you need it sooner," I informed him as I made notes on the alteration tag.

"Naw. That'll be fine."

"Can I get a name, please?"

"Fock. Hugh Fock."

I had never heard this name before but was fairly certain the man wasn't messing with me.

"F-O..." I led off.

"C-K," he finished. "Just like it sounds."

"Just like it sounds," I repeated as I bit into my cheeks, wondering how many times he'd had to repeat his name back and then spell it out in his lifetime. "Will that be cash or charge, Mr. Fock?"

"I have a house account."

At the time, all our in-store charge accounts were listed in a big computer printout book indexed by last name and containing the customer's address and credit limit. $300 was the usual.

"Probably under Hubert Fock."

Sure enough, it was, and with a $500 limit. Impressive.

"Route 9. Uncertain, Texas?"

"That's me."

"Very good."

I prepared the sales ticket and turned the pad around for his signature.

"I sure do thank you, Mr. Fock, and I guess we'll see you next Saturday. I'm Kenzie, by the way. Kenzie Church."

We shook hands.

"Nice to meet you, Kenzie. You Judd's boy?"

"Yessir."

"Yeah, I miss those commercials of his."

"Yessir. He's off playing Hayride most of the time now."

"They got good bean soup out there. Took the wife not long ago."

"Sure do. Fill you up on that, so you don't have as much room for that 'all you can eat' barbecue."

"That's true. But it sure is good. Well, I'll be seein' you."

I didn't know it at the time, but truer words had never been spoken. Hugh Fock gave me a wave and made for the stairs, and I was on the phone in an instant. Scoon Penn was gonna love this.

"Fock?!" Scoon said into the phone way too loudly. I imagined Larry cringing at the word that had to have found its way over the railing of the mezzanine and down onto the main floor. "You're shittin' me," he continued in tones he thought were markedly lower than his previous outburst.

I had an idea, so I hung up fast.

Back in those days, the store had one primary phone number that ended in 6208, along with two other numbers that were used as rollover lines if the first one was busy: 6209 and 6200. I never could figure out why the easier 6200 wasn't the primary number, but it was now the one blinking with someone on hold.

I called up to the office to request a page. Wilda Jean, the office manager, had a large table microphone on her desk that was connected to the Muzak speaker system and could easily broadcast throughout the store. She and the other office ladies referred to the phone lines as Line 8, Line 9 and, for whatever weird reason, "Line Naught." I never liked hearing any page for that number, wishing they would just call it Line Ott or Line Zero. I mean, it sounded like someone was in trouble.

"Hey, Wilda. It's Kenzie. Hey, I just had a suit sale to Mr. Hugh Fock of Uncertain, Texas. Says he has a $500 limit, but you guys told me to call upstairs on house charges, so I'm just making sure."

I waited for her to verify Mr. Fock's credit. I didn't care. It was just part of the ruse that was to follow, a necessary proof that I wasn't playing a joke on her, which I'd been known to do with some regularity. She came back on the line and told me all was well.

"Okay, good. I think he's up front waiting on his car to be brought around and his wife's holding for him on (I grimaced) Line Naught. Can you page him and let him know? I'm stuck down here with another customer. Thanks so much."

The Kraken was about to be released. I smiled and ascended the stairs where my glance to the balcony was met by Scoon's expectant grinning face.

"Mr. Hugh Fock, you have a call on Line Naught." Wilda's voice boomed from the nearby speaker.

Scoon turned bright red, and he was reduced to a silent laugh that he routinely found when incapacitated by something he found too funny to bear.

"Hugh Fock. Line Naught."

Scoon clutched at his belly and rolled to his side, disappearing behind the display wall of shoes. He was done.

Mr. Fock was, in fact, awaiting the valet car service my father had instituted to try and make downtown shopping more convenient for those who still bothered to shop there, and it was a cool thing. No matter if the times dictated we had to have a mall store, the downtown one was our flagship location, like Neiman-Marcus or Macy's and that would never change.

My man Hugh was directed toward the valet desk at the front where the blinking light on the phone was clearly visible. I ducked into the short-sleeve stockroom and canceled the call just as he was about to punch in.

When I made my way back out of hiding, Mr. Fock stood there puzzled and waited an extra ten minutes in that very spot for the call that never came.

I waved when he finally made up his mind to leave, and then returned to my perch at the head of the stairs to await the full reaction of my buddy, Scoon.

"Ol' Hugh Fock was actually pretty cool to me," I offered in defense of my customer when Scoon got within earshot.

"Yeah, me too. I sold him some loafers," Scoon said. "But just hearing that shit over the loudspeaker was priceless. Poor bastard."

Our fun came to a screeching halt when I looked over Scoon's shoulder.

"You two need to hold it down. I could hear you from the top of the stairs." The directive came from the man I called Barbunzo. He was my father's best friend and the general manager of Fleming & Burns.

Millicent Barbunzo Sr. was a likeable fellow. His wife was one of my mother's college friends, and he'd known my dad for as long. When we moved back to Shreveport in 1971, the first thing my father did was beg Millicent to move there, too, from Ohio and help him run the family enterprise. Together, they separately owned the shoe department and leased the space from Fleming & Burns as a way to cut in Barbunzo without actually offering him a share of what would be my inheritance. When my father decided to revive the Hayride in 1974, the job of managing the clothing store fell to Barbunzo until I was sufficiently groomed to assume the throne.

Now, think a moment on what I just said. Has that strategy ever worked for any royal family in history? "Oh, here. You train my son and when you're done, he'll take over, and you'll be out of a job." The short answer: "No."

Millicent Sr. was in no hurry at all for me to assume the throne at Fleming & Burns, and neither was I, but that didn't change Dear Old Dad's plans. This "plan" would factor into my forthcoming relationship with Maezie Fock in ways neither of us could have possibly ever fathomed.

10

"Ni!"

The last thing I wanted was a sunburn. I'd been practicing what I'd always called "good tan management" since arriving in Ecuador, which was funny since my fair skin wasn't very prone to tanning at all, and therefore, should not need any management beyond steering clear of the sun after thirty minutes or 11:00 a.m., whichever came first.

I'd been daydreaming, rereading the same half dozen pages in A Gentleman in Moscow but thinking of Maezie.

I want you to know that I cherish the moments that we've spent together, like a taste of Heaven. I know there is no one else in the world that understands me as you do and, furthermore, I know there is no one else that would take the time to care as you have. I love you, and I want you to understand that every time I say those special words, I mean them even more. The reason I am writing you right now is since we are apart, it is impossible to release emotions that nearly overcome me. You are my life and my inspiration. And my love...and I do so love you.

I stared at the letter Maezie wrote me on my twenty-first birthday. The letter that lived through moves and marriages and crossed continental divides to be beachside at this very moment. And I wondered why the hell her simple and resolute proclamation—my first real glimpse inside the heart of a woman in love—was so unique to my experiences on earth that I hadn't been able to find my way back to them in the many years since. But since my divorce, I'll be goddamned if I'm going to settle for anything less.

The Four Before meant nothing.

The ex, nothing.

Only one person had ever loved me as I'd desired to be loved. And here, today, on the beach in Manta, Ecuador, I was grateful for ever having known Maezie Fock, so I took a moment to pray I would know love like that once again.

I shut my eyes and smiled.

You are my life and my inspiration.

• • •

"It is completely insane how much I love you already," Maezie confessed to me the second week of our union. "That's not normal for me. I don't just fall in love like that."

She studied me, watching as the smile of sheer joy that spread across my face ran out of room and was forced to morph into some sort of sheepish grin, with a side of deviltry to it. I looked something like the Grinch as he contemplated his glorious assault on Whoville Christmas Eve. She returned a better smile, laced with mischief of her own making, and pressed me for comment.

"You're enjoying this, aren't you? Torturing me like this. You ought to be ashamed of yourself, Mackenzie Church!"

"There is no shame," I assured the woman who was undoubtedly my everything. I lowered my chin so I could regard Maezie with a look Flynn Ryder would later label as "The Smolder," but what I was simply trying to pull into service as "The Face of Extreme Sincerity" since we were both given to pranking and unpredictable laughter, albeit rarely at the unexpected volume of my neighbor, Jaycee. "...because I am shamelessly in love with you, too, Maezie."

Sincerity achieved. I didn't have far to reach because Maezie and I usually sat close to each other, if not interlaced like some sort of Celtic knot or Indian mandala. I pulled her to me, and we kissed and kissed again. She had the softest lips, and they always welcomed mine. Maezie Fock was, in every respect I could figure, an extension of me.

I suddenly felt incapacitated, overwhelmed just holding her hands in mine. Maezie was wearing a powder-blue jumper over a white shirt, had two tiny, white bows in her hair, and looked simply angelic.

"Hang on," I said to her as I released her hands and went across the room to my bookshelf.

"Hey!" she came back with, along with that unique pout I spoke of earlier.

"One sec," I said as I leafed through my albums like a madman. "Here we go."

I cued up Track 7 of K-Tel's *Music Explosion* LP on my turntable and let the band Alive & Kickin' take over where words had failed me.

"Listen," I instructed the still-pouting Maezie, as I retook my seat beside her and latched onto her waiting hands. She complied, and understood my intended message that no one else had ever given me such a beautiful feeling. I was deep in unshakeable love. There would be no letting go.

This time I didn't need to sing along. I just watched as the words flowed over Maezie, satisfied I'd expressed myself through music yet again and, perhaps, that would hold me for a bit.

"Hold on," I offered at the conclusion of the chorus. She did, and it was, by all accounts, just a little bit tighter than the time before.

I stood and pulled her to me, and we completed the song with an impromptu slow dance in the tiny space between the door and my bed. It was another beautiful moment, another attempt to celebrate or otherwise confront our shared passion for one another head-on. This energy simply had to go somewhere and "getting physical" as Olivia Newton John tried to convince us she was fully capable of, only further stoked the fires of our hearts. We had to have other expressions: usually just time together, intertwined, touching, reveling in one another. Once again, a song had come to our rescue.

Whatever gentle mood I've invoked here was shattered in the next moment when my other suite mate, Mel, made a loud entrance into the outer hallway with a "Ni!"

Mel had adopted the Monty Python *Knights of Ni* greeting as his way of checking to see if we were in residence behind closed doors without having to knock.

Romantic mood deflated, Maezie and I obliged Mel in unison, "Ni!"

He laughed as we heard him rattle his keys and open his door.

"Ni!" came the softer counter of his girlfriend, Mary, who was herself an expert in how to navigate the fire drills of Cline dormitory.

"Let's get out of here," Maezie said. "You up for a movie?"

"Sure," I agreed. "Anything in particular?"

"The *Halloween* sequel just came out. Let's go get scared!"

And so, we did.

Maezie and I cruised by the school cafeteria to grab a quick bite before heading to the Quail Creek Twin. The

Delta boys had gotten used to seeing us together, inseparable as we were, and some level of animosity was beginning to surface. The chapter's resident clown spent little, if any, time hanging with his buds anymore.

"The hell you been, White Boy?" one of them shouted out as we took our seats at a nearby table, close enough to count as our turf but not right up in the thick of things.

"Busy, dumb shit!" someone else offered, noting my beautiful Maezie.

"You comin' down to the house tonight? We've got a couple of kegs left over from the pledge party. Might even get some porch sliding in."

"Maybe later," I said, failing to convince even myself. "Maezie and I are gonna go catch a movie."

"Yeah, we see what you're catching, puss boy. See you next spring."

What an unnecessary, unsolicited derision. I wasn't expecting this from my "brothers" and didn't know what to say. I could tell Maezie didn't like the teasing, so I suggested we take our leave. We rose.

"Beats the hell out of another Friday night circle jerk," I shot back.

Nobody had anything to say to that dumb comment. Maezie looked miserable as we dropped our trays on the conveyor belt and got the hell out of the cafeteria in a hurry.

"You're gonna have to come up with a better response than that," Maezie chastised me when we were out of earshot. Her dour expression began to change for the better as she regarded me in the parking lot. "Where was that famous Kenzie wit?"

"I wasn't expecting that, Maezie. I'm sorry. I'll lay into them Sunday night at the meeting, 'cause that shit's gotta stop now."

"Tell them you're spoken for and to fuck off!" Maezie exclaimed as she put her arms around me and drew me into what was supposed to be a wonderful kiss but ended up being a snot match as we both laughed at her out-of-character use of profanity. Brilliant timing. God, I loved Maezie, even as we each rushed to be the first to raid the napkin stash in the console.

Every white person in America should attend a black church at least once in their lifetime. It will give them an attitude adjustment, and they will marvel at the unabashed celebration and joy found inside the church's rockin' walls.

Similarly, black folks have a unified, all-consuming reaction when it comes to horror movies, working hard to keep the cast safe by shouting warnings and unsolicited advice at the screen in some vain attempt to change the tragic outcome unfolding before them.

Maezie and I found we were decidedly in the minority as *Halloween 2* got underway.

The Quail Creek Twin had only recently been converted into a fourplex by simply removing a few seats and inserting a dividing wall down the middle of their two theaters. Trouble was, the seating was curved in a semi-circle around the central screen that was now gone, so you faced at maybe a twenty-two-degree angle away from the screen, which only added to the sense of disorientation the scary music was trying to invoke. We were toward the back, on one of the short rows on the left, sitting almost sideways.

"Watch it, girl!" someone shouted from the center aisle of the darkened theater. "Naw! Hell, naw! Don't sit down like that! Get up!"

"Here he comes!" another concerned theater goer warned from somewhere behind us.

"Move y'ass! Run!"

Even though Maezie and I had been made painfully aware of what was coming, we both jumped when Michael Myers came into frame in his trademark mask.

I guess during their haste to finish the theater "modifications" before that night's show—their premiere—the ownership of the new Quail Creek Cinema 4 had forgotten their final walk-through. I was clutching the left armrest, now over my head. "Oh, shit."

Maezie's eyes became the most delightful crescents, as I jimmied the armrest back in place.

"I haven't laughed like that in a long time," Maezie managed as she tried not to disappear into her own version of the famous Scoon Penn silent laugh. We were finally eating dinner at Sorrel's Café, or at least, trying. I let Maezie eat most of the Captain's Wafers because they seemed to make her even happier. There was just something about a squirt of Green Goddess dressing and those crackers that was good and tasty and cheap. We split what the menu called the Monster Chicken Fried Steak, and our waitress offered no response when I asked her if "monster" described the chicken or the resulting portion.

I think we sat there longer than we did in the movie, grateful for good food and good company, and slowly calming down from the evening's excitement.

When we finally got up to leave, I couldn't resist one more reminder of our movie adventure.

"Move y'ass, girl!" I said to Maezie in a louder voice but nothing like what we'd just experienced.

"Be sure and leave a good tip," Maezie countered. "And the armrest too."

The crescents were back. Such a treasure.

11

Uncertain

The following weekend, I accompanied Maezie back home to Uncertain, Texas. After my Sunday night lashing out at the Delta boys, giving them a suitable haranguing that began with "If you truly gave a shit about me..." and went from there, we decided a little time away from campus was in order. And it was time, anyway, to meet the parents.

Maezie had confirmed with her dad that he was, in fact, the same Hugh Fock I'd waited on at Fleming & Burns the previous year (some sort of foreshadowing, I'd like to think). So I was somewhat of a known quantity to him at least, but I'd never been to the scene of his alleged bovine assault, nor had the pleasure of meeting the woman responsible for birthing and naming my precious gal.

There's not much to Uncertain, Texas. Wasn't back then either. For the most part, it was a small lakeside town in a bend in the road of what is essentially East Texas pastureland and piney woods. Don Henley of the *Eagles* lived around there somewhere, and while Caddo Lake was the big attraction, and Johnson's Ranch Marina served as the de facto gathering spot of the local "who's who," the Fock residence was located down Route 9 a ways, in what was probably Karnack. But where would you rather be, a town with the great name of Uncertain or a lesser one that evokes memories of a turban clad Johnny Carson? I will say this, though, Karnack has an old-timey general store that I believe was featured in some Disney movie—and it was truly a time warp on the inside. Oh, and Karnack was the birthplace of Claudia Alta Taylor Johnson, better known as Lady Bird, the outspoken wife of President Lyndon Baines Johnson.

"We're here," Maezie announced presently.

I looked to the right and, sure enough, there was the red barn from her drawing.

"Nice barn-shed-thing," I said. "Where're the cows?"

"Slaughtered. Every last one of them."

"Wrenches?"

"Sledgehammers."

We laughed, then I noticed a different kind of funny feeling in my stomach as we untangled ourselves and exited the Riviera. I was actually quite nervous.

Belinda was wiping down the kitchen counter when we entered the house through the garage door without knocking. This was, after all, Maezie's home too.

"You could've at least used the front door, Maezie," her mother mildly scolded as she dried her hands and primped in anticipation of meeting the new boy in her daughter's life.

According to the government, I was now of draft age, so I suppose I could be called a 'man,' but I felt more like a boy, a little boy, as I stood trial before one of the gatekeepers.

"The garage was closer," Maezie tossed back.

"Please forgive my daughter," Belinda said to me, determined to take charge of the critical intro that was taking too long for her liking. "Pleased to meet you," she continued, shoving her right hand past Maezie.

"This is Kenzie," Maezie assisted. "And this is my mother, Belinda."

We smiled and mumbled further greetings amid the second iteration of apologies for the state of what appeared to be a fairly well-kept garage.

Belinda was not overly tall, maybe 5'4" or so, and I could see where Maezie got the ability to contort her eyes into fun li'l crescents, even though her mom kept hers partially obscured behind round glasses with rather formidable tortoise shell rims. Oh, and out came the dimples as she smiled. Having previously met Hugh, I was thankful Maezie had inherited mostly her mother's looks in the blending process of her conception. Hugh was there, though, somewhere in that wondrous pout of hers, for sure.

"Hello, you," Belinda continued, turning to greet the daughter she hadn't seen in a month of Sundays. Literally.

Maezie hugged her mama, then grabbed for an apple from the bowl on the counter and wasted no time taking a big bite.

"Where's Dad?"

"He called and said he was gonna be a little late. Something to do with the epolyne levels." Belinda looked my way to clarify. "I don't understand all that business."

"Dad works for Texas Eastman," Maezie reminded me, even though I'd already committed that fact to memory.

"Yeah, we pass that place on the highway on the way to clothing market in Dallas. I call it The Industrial City. Smells like whiskey sour candy when you drive by," I tossed out for something to contribute in my nervousness.

"It does look pretty at night, all lit up," Belinda confirmed.

I could tell she found no favor in the "whiskey sour" comment, even if it was only a candy, for heaven's sake. It seemed I was already being assessed for addition to the naughty list and we weren't even five minutes along.

"It *does* smell like whiskey sour candy," Maezie jumped in, as if my observation had been the missing piece she had been seeking in her own mind. And, she'd unintentionally bailed me out of jail with her mom as I watched Belinda struggle with who now to assess in that shifting moment.

I didn't notice I was standing there with my hands jammed in my windbreaker until Maezie looped an arm through mine and began taking me on a tour of the home.

Her action amid an economy of words was not lost on Mama B. Whatever was being communicated between those two, whomever Belinda had begun to assess, was now part of a package deal.

"I have Kenzie set up in the guest room," Belinda unnecessarily mentioned as the initial interview period was being marked "done" by our departure.

I was hardly expecting to bunk in Maezie's room and was, therefore, caught off guard when Maezie nudged me as she replied to the air, "Thank you, Mama."

I bit my cheeks and tried to immerse myself in the photos that lined the walls. The tour of Casa Fock had begun. Vacant eyes of long-dead farmers and other people I had yet to learn the names of stared back at me. Gentle smiles from supportive women told me this generation of Focks was perhaps managing their stead with a little more comfort than those who'd come before.

Belinda sorted a few into "my husband's people," and the rest I was left to assume were hers. A "yes, Mother" from Maezie firmly concluded the genealogy portion, and we were left to carry on solo.

"Hicks and hayseeds," Maezie muttered in summation, and that was that.

Hubert Shale Fock looked pretty beat when he arrived at the last possible second before grace.

Belinda had received an update but was only going to wait so long to serve the evening meal and had begun setting the table with the makings of a good home-cooked dinner as soon as she had hung up with him. "He can just heat his up," I was told, and understood this to mean it was not the first or last time the epolyne levels had gone out of whack at Texas Eastman.

"Hey. Good to see you again," he offered as I stood and shook his hand. "Still got the suit. Fits like a dream." Hugh took his seat and was immediately on the receiving end of a bowl of mashed potatoes. He wasted no time filling his plate. "Funny how you two ended up knowing each other. School and all."

I was braced for the "how serious are you about her, boy?" comment but Hugh chose to dig into a chicken thigh instead, and the matter never came up. Not in that initial conversation, at least.

We talked some more on Fleming & Burns and my dad, and if I'd met any famous people on the Louisiana Hayride show. What was probably close to an hour of conversation passed rather quickly, and I was somewhat relieved when Hugh stood up and announced he was pulling for the undefeated Texan Randy Cobb that night in his bout with boxing legend Ken Norton.

"I don't care a lick for his language, but the boy sure knows how to fight. Not sure what time exactly it starts," Hugh added as he folded his napkin and began clearing his plate.

"Well, hopefully, we'll be back in time for the start," Maezie interjected as she eyed me with a grin.

"Where are you two headed?" Belinda genuinely wanted to know.

"On a walk."

As long as my Riviera stayed put, this seemed an agreeable alternative to Mr. and Mrs. Fock.

I thanked Belinda for the nice meal. I was truly stuffed, having gone well beyond the boundaries of simple politeness in portions consumed, and welcomed any opportunity to work off some of the tonnage the meal had imbued upon my modest frame.

Arm inserted once more in mine, Maezie shared the same silent conversation with her dad I'd witnessed earlier with Mama Belinda, and we took our leave, this time through the front door. I was to learn the parents, in her opinion, had been handled.

12

Pea Ridge

"Curt, baaahh-we, why do you do these things?"

Lena Mae Anderson was upset about something, though I no longer remember what. It was her extreme Southern drawl that left its impact on me on that sweltering summer day in 1977 as I witnessed her trying to lecture my second-tier friend, her son, Curt Anderson. I think maybe she'd busted him, yet again, for dipping Skoal, which he was just always gonna do. At times, Lena's drawl could outdo my mother's. Only at times, though, because although my mother was born and raised in Shreveport, you'd think the city was somewhere south of Savannah from the way she made certain words into standalone sentences. I only knew Lena Mae a few brief years before cancer claimed her too young and explained why she'd had so little energy all those times she'd tried to get her kids to behave.

I called Curt my second-tier friend because I really didn't start spending a lot of time with him until Mr. Nabe, who could be a real asshole at times because he essentially was, got pissed at my dad for getting pissed at him and said some stupid shit on the phone that made Judd issue an edict, stating I was to no longer be friends with the Nabe boys or hang at their house after school. This was tragic. Mike and his brother, Ben, formed the core of my neighborhood gang and were solely responsible for guiding me away from platform heels and groovy knit pants to .22s and dirt bikes.

How do parents just unilaterally do that? So, the Nabes had been "unfriended" by my dad in the many decades before Facebook gave rise to the term, and I had to find other guys to play with after school—unless I felt like riding my bike the three plus miles to Scoon Penn's house, which I rarely did. That meant the Anderson boys, Curt and occasionally Cary, but never the youngest, nerdy Dalton, or the Welch brothers, whose mom was a wonderful and nice lady, but the dad was an out-of-control narcissist who moonlighted as a deacon in the Baptist church and tried to enforce uber-Christian dogma on his family and anyone within earshot, even though he failed to uphold those standards for himself.

Hanging with Prentiss and Rick Welch could be fun—they had a trampoline and a real fireman's pole from their playroom down to the laundry room below, and I had a crush on their gentle and beautiful mom, but the Welchs and the Nabes had some sort of war going on, started by Asshole Nabe, who'd water his tomato plants while drinking scotch, a ruse to monitor the comings and goings of his next-door neighbors while instructing his free-range dog to go shit in their yard right when "The Deacon," as he called Mr. Welch, arrived home.

Mr. Nabe referred to Deacon Welch's boys as Penis and Dick, which I thought ironic since his first name was actually Dick, and he was the personification of any salacious innuendo associated with that moniker. But I also found it hilarious.

Curt Anderson was a couple of years younger than me and had long hair before any of us were allowed to or thought it necessary as some sort of rebellious expression. Curt was all about rebellious expression. He attended a Catholic boys' school and wasn't home five minutes each afternoon before Led Zeppelin was blaring from the speakers in his room, and he was perched at his drum set playing along, dip cup at his feet, the bed littered with all manner of comic books. It wasn't easy to motivate Curt to venture outside his room once entrenched, except maybe to fish the neighborhood pond that abutted his backyard, so I knew if I dropped in on him, I was most likely in for hard rock music and perusing comic books for a few hours.

To his credit, Curt was a good drummer, and we had a good enough time together, especially once his new neighbor, a buxom blonde, began gardening in low-cut tops in the flower bed while pretending to be oblivious to our blatant second-story window gawking. We hung out a couple of years until, at seventeen, Curt got a girl pregnant and went off to build a life with her. I remember being his only real friend when all that went down. There's still a picture of me handing him a ten-dollar bill floating around somewhere. It was to pay the Justice of the Peace for their wedding because he hadn't thought to grab some cash before heading out to that blessed event.

Curt and I talked about life a lot and decided that the development of the sixty-acre field at the back of the neighborhood was an abomination as it would put an end to all our motorcycle and go-cart trails and would make the neighborhood drive-through-able. But workers had already filled in the weird overgrown pond with the dark and strange looking goggle-eyed fish we were convinced were a prehistoric and forgotten species, so all our wishing in the world proved futile. City life was beginning to encroach, and anything to do with the upcoming 1980s just sounded gross to us.

Curt and I had a saying, part of the lexicon we were developing line by line for our little cadre we'd taken to calling the Pea Ridge Bawys, in honor of his recently departed mother. Some days, we would draw out the word for ten seconds or more, running out of breath before the imitation of "boys" was concluded. Other days, the word rhymed with "wowee," and we seemed to like that just fine.

The neighborhood was actually Pepper Ridge, named for the Pepper family that built the first home in the 1930s and operated what later became the Whoop & Holler Boys Camp for a time once they built Shreveport's first swimming pool just prior to World War II. We called it "P. Ridge" or "Pea Ridge." It was a cool place to grow up, I've gotta say.

So, the new saying Curt and I developed came from one of our many weekend camping trips to the nearby cotton fields. We had this one spot under a big oak tree, close to the highway, where we could hide out, build a bonfire, and still feel like we were in the country while also being able to take our bikes a couple of miles into town to boost more comic books and candy from the local Pak-A-Sak when they weren't looking. I mean, if they didn't question why we were wearing ski jackets in near-sixty-degree weather, they deserved to lose a little inventory, especially given we actually paid the ridiculous full price for their frozen drinks known as Icees. Thirty-five cents! Pirates!

The next morning, Curt and I would awake to find our mouths painted in some sort of chalky unpleasantry that he described as socks on our teeth with a "Kenz, my teeth are coated." From then on, anything gross was "coated."

Our dictionary was just beginning to take form when the whole "hey, I gotta go get married and be a dad" thing happened. That, and the time Curt shot me in the arm during church, contributed to his slow fade from my life in the months ahead.

Sunday mornings back then were ghost towns for kids seeking to carry over their Saturday morning weekend cartoon binges. You might could catch some Christian slanted cartoon like *Davey & Goliath* or something wholesome like *The New Zoo Review*, but you could forget about *Johnny Quest* or *Scooby Doo* or the *Looney Tunes* bunch.

Curt and I were back from camping early one Sunday, and he wasn't ready to go home yet, so he was flipping the dial on the small black-and-white TV in my room while we ate leftover pizza. He paused on televangelist Rex Humbard for some unknown reason and that prompted me to ask if he'd given up searching for the elusive *Bullwinkle* that occasionally showed up on Sunday mornings on one of the UHF channels.

Curt had been busying himself by pumping up my Crosman BB gun and firing it around the room. We both knew it was empty because we'd exhausted the chamber the night before on a whole wall of soda cans and bottles back at the campsite.

"Check this out," he said as he fired one off at his forearm, and I watched as the skin briefly pushed aside like ripples from some rock landing in a pond. "Feels weird."

So, Curt did another one pump, pointed it at my left bicep and fired from an inch away. It did, in fact, feel weird as the compressed air distorted the skin on my arm, but then it began to hurt like hell. I looked at Curt, and he was already turning pale as blood began to trickle from my now substantially aching arm.

"Oh, shit!" he exclaimed.

"I better go tell the Supreme Madré," I said, referencing the name he and I'd come up with for my mother, who always had the last word and who always must be obeyed.

"I'm gonna bail," Curt said rather suddenly as he opened the outside door my father had thought to add to my room during one of the remodels though I hardly deserved the vote of confidence.

"You don't have to leave. It's no big deal," I said to the closed door. But Curt was gone, and I went to find the Supreme One for my confession, leaving Rex Humbard preaching to an empty room.

As the ER doctor would inform my parents a short time later in a lecture vocalized solely for my benefit, "This could have been a big deal. You're lucky, son, the BB lodged an eighth of an inch from an artery. Best just to leave it alone. Not harming anything, and we don't want to risk nerve damage."

And so, I survived being shot "during church," and to this day, I still set off certain overly sensitive airport screening devices. And, yes, my father then "unfriended" the Andersons over that little episode. But I was now of driving age, and the Nabe boys and Scoon and I were back thick as thieves. Within a month or so, Curt was gone from my life and my second-tier friend group dissolved into thin air as I hadn't seen the Welch brothers for a few years since the birthday for Prentiss out at the airport where we got to meet real airline pilots, sit in the cockpit of a 727, and were given real looking model planes as take-home gifts.

Soon after, I believe The Deacon lost everything gambling somewhere and got kicked out of the church, because the Welchs ended up moving and the parents got divorced.

Dick Nabe died a few years later at the early age of fifty-six of complications from being an asshole. I'm sure his chain smoking and scotch drinking didn't help matters either. The dog, the fifth in a long series of beagles in the Nabe family, all named "Poochie," continued to shit in the Welch's yard until it was her turn to die.

13

Trip

Once my father made up his mind to leave the daily grind of Fleming & Burns behind and return to his roots in radio, his whole world changed. Gone were the snappy and stylish suits, traded in for faded blue jeans and cheap western shirts with fake pearl-colored snap closures, which he'd purchase at K-Mart.

I kid you not.

What would his downtown fans think if they were to find out? We simply did not discuss the matter around the Church household, my mother and I choosing to look the other way as one might forgive a farmer whose overalls smelled of manure from an honest day's toil. But, oh, the shame. Especially given this was the era of Vegas Elvis and the sequined outfits, and my father often sought to enlist both of us to hold shirt collars and epaulettes while he crimped silver stars in place or added the umpteenth rhinestone to the already over-gaudy outfit he would host the show in that coming Saturday.

While I love the lyrics from the Glen Campbell song "Rhinestone Cowboy," and the way he sings it, whenever I hear it, I have nightmarish flashbacks to those outfits my father wore on stage. Thank god Elvis passed away shortly thereafter—before my father thought to add a trove of scarves to his ensemble. More than once, I caught him eyeing those oversized belt contraptions only Elvis could get away with—because when it came to western belt buckles, normally bigger meant better.

The rest of the adult male population had little room to talk. Leisure suits were all the rage at Fleming & Burns during this blip of fashion faux pas, and I was working overtime just trying to keep the ridiculously thin and colorful nylon tops I called "slime shirts" from walking out the front door layered inside someone's pants. That particular fad lasted five or six very taxing years, and I was glad to see it fade into rightful oblivion at the end of the disco era.

• • •

My father grew up the youngest of three boys in Virginia, born on the outskirts of Roanoke in a wooded area showing up on only a few moonshiner maps as Bent Mountain. Appalachia, for all that descriptor conjures for you. Middle brother, Gordon, died of tetanus from an accidental gunshot wound that I suspect my father and his other brother had something to do with. I thought it was his service in World War II that had messed Papa up, but I saw later the damage ran deeper.

Gordon was barely nine when the accident report was written up by his grandfather, Big Mac, who happened to be a Roanoke police officer and may have adjusted the facts to fit the narrative being spun on Bent Mountain. At the Church household, the resulting blame settled on Mackenzie Jr., or "Rowe" as most folks called him, even though he was tending his job as a train conductor on the Great Northern railway when the shooting occurred.

Rowe liked to drink, a lot, and apparently was at least verbally, if not physically, abusive to his wife most nights as my father recalled. Big Mac was disappointed in his one and only son and figured leaving the boys to their own devices had led to the mischief that ultimately cost Gordon his life.

That untimely death, combined with the start of the Great Depression the following month, proved too much for Rowe's bride, a single room schoolteacher with the amazing birth name of California Gold Light. Truth, people. Gold, as she was mercifully known, filed for divorce and was strong enough to raise my father and his older brother, Howard, on up to adulthood. "Trip" as Howard had always called his little brother, had a bit of a detour along the way.

By the summer of 1938, Howard had left the nest and was looking forward to what would be the only year of college at the University of Virginia his scholarship would cover. Gold, needing every moment of relaxation the three-month summer break could give her, decided to ship Trip off to visit his cousins in New York City.

"That'll give him an adventure," she reasoned. "Mind your manners, Mackenzie," she demanded from the train platform in a final attempt to infuse some maturity into her youngest, who was already approaching six feet tall.

"Of course, Mother," he replied.

Everything about Mackenzie Church III was already proper and just, at least by all outward appearances. Gold had recognized his unusual intelligence early on, and after Rowe had been dismissed, my father had become her shadow. Gold tutored him and answered his every question about homework well above his assigned level. By the end of the first year, Gold had the seven-year-old helping her grade papers. Trip proved himself quite the prodigy, graduating high school the week before the New York excursion, which was, in fact, all Gold could manage as a reward for the boy so quickly becoming a man. He was barely fifteen and excited as hell to disappear into a world so very removed from the only one he'd ever known.

As the story was recounted often to reporters in later years, a cousin's dad worked at Radio City Music Hall as some sort of stage help, and he invited the boys to work with him one day to listen quietly to some of the radio dramas taking place in the extensive studio complex. At some point, someone failed to show for their one-liner as a policeman so the dad, noting my future father's mature sounding voice (and wanting to play the bigshot, no doubt), volunteered him for the job.

Squealing with delight, Trip snatched the script, was directed to his proper spot, choked his emotions down when the moment arrived and uttered his one line with surprising lilt and perfection. The balance of that day and, indeed, the week, flew by as Trip glided from stage to stage, the king of one-liners, willing to clop shoes or slam a door for sound effects or just anything to stay in the game. He was smitten.

When he received his first actual paycheck at the end of week one, Trip was floored that he'd actually been paid to have such fun, not to mention it was darn good money! It was shaping up to be one hell of a vacation. By the end of the month, he'd expanded to featured then leading roles and had already banked the equivalent of his mother's annual salary when it came time to prepare for the return to Roanoke.

"You don't want to overstay your welcome," Gold had cautioned him.

Trip wrote home that very night, bubbling with excitement.

A couple of friends of mine have invited me to stay with them, at least until I can find a place of my own. They're starting their own theater company and want me to be part of their troupe!

Gold didn't know the two young men my father had fallen in with but trusted his judgment in the matter. What harm could there be in another month or two, especially given the money the boy was making and sending home to help out.

You'd like John, Mother. Trip wrote. *He's a good businessman, and Orson is super intelligent and ambitious. I just know they're going to be successful.*

My father's two roommates turned out to be John Houseman and Orson Welles, and their little theater company was to be called the Mercury Theater on the Air. Yes, both were to be wildly successful, and Trip would find himself in the history books as well for just doing the job he now loved more than anything, this time playing three different parts in the infamous *War of the Worlds* radio drama that panicked part of the nation, lit up the switchboards at Radio City, drove the FCC mad, and earned Trip his own apartment—with manservant, all before the real world war got underway in Europe.

I can't even imagine what it must've been like to be making $500 a month back when such a sum could easily buy an automobile, much less having late-night skull sessions with roomies Orson and John or being directed in the Lux Theater programs by none other than Cecil B. DeMille. But such was the place my father found himself in as the 1930s drew to a close.

He'd also outpaced the entire year's earnings of his father, who was apparently remarried and expecting to be a parent again. And he'd even sent some "fun money" home for Howard, so he could "live it up" at college. But this was the big city, the big time, and the war in Europe was getting pretty out of hand. Trip began to yearn for the simpler life, where he could sleep in every once in a while, instead of just Sundays, and have a whole lot less responsibilities upon his not-yet-fully developed shoulders. He missed the creeks and trails of Bent Mountain, and he missed Gold.

One Saturday afternoon as the sun began its descent, my father scored a healthy hit in a pickup game of stickball in the alley behind the studios and was taking a dangerous lead off the rock representing first base when his cousin's dad shouted for him. Trip turned to see the man waving frantically, and he looked angry. Billy-something took his place at first and Trip trotted over, sweaty but all smiles.

"What's up, Mr. Earl? You need something?"

"What I need, Trip, is for you to carry your ass inside! Rehearsal started fifteen minutes ago, and the director is livid! Sent me to find you. I am not your goddamn babysitter!"

Mr. Earl shouted the rest of his pronouncement at Trip's back as the boy hightailed it inside and executed the world's fastest sink bath and costume change before running on stage with shoes in hand as the rest of the cast returned to their places in preparation for the thunder they knew was coming.

"Mackenzie Church!" the director shouted, addressing the cast. "A boy no longer content to be the new kid on the block. Now one of the precious Mercury players who apparently fancies himself Boy Impresario, ready to manage each of your careers and guide your presence upon the airwaves as he sees fit. Radio be damned! There's a stickball game afoot. All else will keep...it will keep."

Cecil B. DeMille shifted his focus now to Trip and bored into him with all the contempt he could muster. His balding head wrinkled in a torrent of folds, giving the impression of multiple eyebrows arched in anger.

"Time waits for no man, Mr. Church, much less a boy caught up in his own little world without regard for his fellow actors or the job at hand. Rehearsal was scheduled to begin promptly at 7:00 p.m., allowing those lacking in the mastery of their craft ample time to bring their standards in line with your lofty ones. But it is now quarter past the hour and not the first word has been uttered, for those words are assigned to you this evening as someone's unfortunate choice for the lead in our production. I err but once on your behalf, Mr. Church. What do you have to offer the cast for your wanton disregard? The stage is yours."

Sure, Trip Church was smart, sure he could act, but he had holes in his armor, big ones, and he knew it. He'd apparently overstayed his welcome in the big city and yearned for something far less complicated, something resembling a normal childhood—though he confessed to himself he had little idea what that might look like.

"I, uh, got caught up in the game and lost track of time, sir. I'm sorry, everyone. I guess sometimes the kid in me takes over. I'm truly sorry, sir." Trip regarded his director when he uttered this last apology. "Can we start now? I think there's still time."

My father had done the best job he knew how to do, offered the best apology he could think of with a stomach that threatened to broadcast its contents far and wide if things didn't settle down in a hurry.

Director DeMille regarded him as something less than human in that frozen moment. "So, your excuse to Mrs. Marchand and Mr. Taylor, to Bunny and Carol and Steve and Owen is 'sorry, I was acting like a kid?' That's all you have to say for yourself?"

"No, sir. I—it won't happen again—"

"You can be goddamn certain of that, Mr. Church!" DeMille bellowed, having reached the crescendo of his verbal assault. "You were irresponsible to the highest order and fully guilty of acting not in the capacity of the mature leader of tonight's assembled troupe but, rather, like nothing more than a fucking kid."

Even though Cecil DeMille's final expletive had trailed off to something barely audible to most of the assembled cast—as he stormed off toward who-knows-where to have a shot or at least insert some sort of break in which to calm down—my father had heard it loud and clear. And it resonated with him to his core.

He took but a moment to check his feelings before proceeding with what he knew was the igniting of the bridge that had brought him thus far in his radio career.

"That's because I *am* a fucking kid," Trip stated clearly with all the conviction he could muster.

After the resplendent and immensely satisfying echo had died down, Cecil B. DeMille turned and regarded my badass future papa—who was already wondering what time the train left for Roanoke in the morning.

"Well played, Mr. Church," he delivered flatly but with the slightest smirk challenging the corners of his pursed lips. "I shall always remember your swan song."

14

The Supreme Madré

A lot of what I know about my father's history is a mix of fact and fiction, swirled together like the story depicted in the Albert Finney movie *Big Fish*.

Judd Church wasn't very vocal about his past as a general rule, preferring to cherry pick it for whatever elements he needed in the moment to make his point or lend some credibility to whatever opinion he might be expressing. I took up genealogy when my daughter was born because I wanted to pass along the family history he never would share, blaming the trauma of battle for his tight lips on World War II and blaming everything else on being raised without a dad from age six on. The "no father figure" excuse was his go-to crutch whenever I pressed him on his lack of involvement in my life, so I eventually gave up trying to change or understand him any more than I did.

As I got older and had to, at times, merge, rearrange, or inflate events to suit whatever resumé I was crafting, I came to realize my father had filled in some gaps in his own way too. It would take me decades after his passing to finally gain a clear picture of the man with the same name but for the Roman numeral suffix, and I was pleased to find he told the truth in an order that made sense to him, much like the quatrains left behind by Nostradamus. I just had to learn his thought processes.

Judd wasn't much of a factor in my life during the time Maezie and I began dating. In fact, he was basically opposed to my attending college at all, having already determined my future like some sort of arranged marriage. My creative mind and spirit fought him at every turn and prevailed until I passed the four-year mark with no degree, and he called "game over," whether I was done with it or not.

Every Friday and Saturday night found my mother at home alone, watching *Murder, She Wrote* or *Fantasy Island* on the satellite dish, reading any number of mystery and biography books at the same time while drinking endless cups of coffee and munching on star peppermints, which she always kept in the pockets of her housecoat along with tissues and her Lucky Strike "after dinner" cigarettes.

"Judd the Hayride Stud" as I derisively called him, freely knocking his jean-clad stage persona, was doing his showman thing on the weekends and wouldn't materialize until well after midnight either night. He was in his element, doing what he loved while trying to find the next singing sensation in those lean years before *Star Search* showed up on television.

I tried not to think of my mother sitting home alone, and my life at Centenary mostly kept me occupied, especially when Maezie came into it and consumed most every waking thought. But it hadn't been too many years since the triple funeral that none of the Churches had dealt with properly, if at all, and my heart ached at times for the hand that had been dealt to the one I jokingly but reverently called "the Supreme Madré."

One Saturday night not long into our courtship, a few weeks after the quick trip to Uncertain, I asked Maezie if we could run out to Pepper Ridge so she could meet the woman I told all those colorful stories about and witness for herself the slowest, most pronounced Southern drawl of anyone in the state of Louisiana. She quickly agreed and offered me a smile I wished I could've framed and kept forever.

There are too many photos today—what the booth looked like before I sat down to eat, what I had to eat, the cat that slept by the register, selfies of fat and happy diners—every last detail documented and tossed into a "cloud" most people don't even know how to find. Oh, the photos I wish I had, but disposable cameras were just coming on the scene back then, and who lugged one of those around everywhere "just in case"? And then having to wait eons until you took all twenty-four or thirty-six pictures in a roll before turning them in to be developed. Torture!

I was immensely proud of and incalculably in love with Maezie and couldn't wait to show her off to my mother. I sensed Madré would be pleased to know her boy had finally found footing in the dating world after missing out on what should've been my senior year of high school, fumbling around as a junior while I tried, and barely succeeded, at graduating in three years, mostly just to show my father that I could do anything his stupid Hayride stars decided to do.

If Maezie had any fear or trepidation at meeting my gentle mother, she didn't show it when she slid herself to me in the front seat of the Riviera and buckled her body and my right arm into place for the twenty-minute ride south on Highway 1.

"Law-urd, I didn't know you were coming!" my mother greeted us at the door after I finally got the house alarm to shut up. My key had worked, but she'd had the alarm set for the night, and I messed up the code a couple of times before getting it right. Madré looked from me to Maezie and was pleased to find my gal's crescent eyes friendly and welcoming.

"I'm Maezie," she offered ahead of any introduction I was still working out in my nervous mind.

"Low-rain," my mother replied as they shook hands and exchanged brief pleasantries. Then Maezie almost jumped out of her skin when a booming voice from the monitoring station came over a central speaker somewhere inside the house.

"This is WorldNet Security. Please identify yourself."

Apparently, I had not been quick enough for "Mission Control" as I often called them.

"Mackenzie Church. Sorry about that."

Shit. I knew what was coming next.

"Thank you, Mr. Church. Password, please."

All I could do was shake my head as I mumbled the only thing that was going to make this man go away. "Fur Face."

"Thank you, Mr. Church. Enjoy the rest of your evening."

"And thank *you*," I replied with weakened sarcasm.

I looked over at Maezie, who was well into one of Scoon's silent laughs, so I pleaded in vain to my mother.

"Why not the cat's name?"

"Rumpole? Too easy to guess."

"I don't think that guy gives too many chances, Madré."

"Please excuse the mess," my mother said to Maezie, totally dismissing me as she turned and started walking back to the den from whence a proper interrogation was waiting to be had. "The Canning Kitchen"—the room we'd entered from the driveway, an all-gas addition to the central kitchen that was supposed to serve as prep space for all the fresh fruits and vegetables we'd be gathering from our extensive garden (never happened)—was actually in perfect order. Madré's comment was meant to brace Maezie for the condition of the den, specifically the area surrounding my mother's well-worn, gold velveteen chair and mismatched brown footstool.

Few people I knew were prepared to see stacks of magazines and catalogs, each two feet high and numbering in the hundreds, outside a library setting. Make that the receiving room of a library, because even they maintain a sense of decorum and organization to the world at large. But that presentation was somehow eclipsed by my mother's emotional need for—or handy access to—every publication she'd received for the last six months or better. She was a firm believer that if you didn't buy something from *Publisher's Clearinghouse*, they would throw your sweepstakes entries in the trash. Suffice it to say, the Prize Patrol van never darkened the driveway at 2001 Pepper Ridge Drive, despite my mother making up her face for the day in anticipation of said event. No giant cardboard checks were ever proffered her way by Ed McMahon, Dick Clark or anyone else for that matter, but you are welcome to take over the remains of her subscription to *New York* magazine that's still running some fourteen years after her departure from this world.

Maezie took it all in and was careful I was the only one who heard her gasp. I could tell some facet of my being had been called into question and was now ruminating about in that delicious mind of hers, hopefully to be counteracted by whatever words I could offer in antidote after our visit, which I knew had now been prematurely shortened from its planned length.

Mounds of catalogs, magazines, and junk mail from the *Clearinghouse* encircled Madré's chair and ottoman like a moat, and I still don't know how she negotiated the daily defined slivers of oriental rug that comprised the walk space to and from her station without waxing her ass. Factor in the family cat, and I wouldn't want to be the actuary quoting the numbers on that insurance policy.

I kept expecting to hear one of those "I've fallen, and I can't get up!" cries from my mother at any time, but they somehow never came—although I did buy her one of those buttons to wear around her neck on a chain in case it ever did, and she actually wore the damn thing, at least on the weekends when Judd the Hayride Stud was at his version of a star-spangled rodeo.

"I've got to get in here and do something," my mother continued as I pointed toward the couch beyond, and we began assessing our path to it...and our odds of actually making it there.

My father had a beautiful cordovan leather chair and matching footstool that was his station, where he ate dinner on a tray balanced on the arms of his throne. And my mother had her zone. But Maezie and I were relegated to a piece of furniture I truly don't know how the family came to own. Not only did it argue with the other furnishings of the den and outright clash with the glass top fish tank coffee table—now a habitat for an ungrateful cactus and tiny African violets from the *Clearinghouse*—it didn't match the refinement of every other item of furniture our family had possessed since bartering for my crib in those dark days when the earth was still cooling.

Okay, so yeah, I didn't really expound on the other kitchen which was one of those paneled jobs you see in every vintage shot from the late '60s, but there were no gold or avocado or rust-colored appliances in our home. They were white or, perhaps, covered to match the paneling. The couch—oh, god, I can feel it scratching me even now! I swear the damn thing was upholstered in burlap—rust over avocado green, no less, and the cushions had all the give of the exam tables at the vet's office, and all the warmth. Why it was present in the room, I have no idea, and the years of my lying prostrate upon it in an attempt to place my body under the cloud of cigarette smoke that hung down from the ceiling to the three-foot level when both parents were lit up like the smokestacks of Texas Eastman—only there were no pretty lights and it didn't smell like whiskey sour candy and Hugh Fock wasn't battling epolyne levels somewhere in the room—all that lying about I did purely out of self-preservation did nothing to soften the couch into anything bearable.

There is a custom in Hawaii where the homeowners will place a fresh pineapple on the made-up bed of their guests as a gentle signal when it's time to leave. The couch Maezie and I now found ourselves on was the furniture equivalent of that pineapple, and I sensed her rumination had gone to some other level, and I was going to need one hell of an antidote on the ride home.

I tuned back into what my mother was saying, her hand waving broadcasts to enhance her words in case we missed something. Her rants were like soap operas, though, in that you could drift away for a period of time and drift back and still have a pretty good idea of what was going on. I watched, during her soliloquy, as Madré's eyes dipped for only a moment to something at couch level. I silently prayed she was finally rethinking the burlap and the color choice. When I did manage to glance down, I saw both of Maezie's arms entwined around one of mine, both hands clasping mine as their genuine mates. I melted in that moment, seeing the object of my mother's curiosity and feeling unmitigated pride at who I was and who I had at my side.

I was possessed, a claim had been staked, and a much larger silent statement than I had witnessed with either Belinda or Hugh was being received by the Supreme One. Or it was just Maezie possessing me as we had come to do. Either way, I was fine with the expression that would now stand in defiance of every bad memory I had ever had upon that crappy couch. I saw my mother visibly relax and smile as she drew out her arm movements to match the meter of her drawn out speech.

Maezie laughed, not out of politeness but because my mother could be genuinely funny if you immersed yourself in one of her oratory events, and my precious gal had. She was rapt in her attention, generous with her crescents, and overpowering with her sincere and beautiful smile. She even tried to match one of my mother's sweeping hand gestures during her own moment of storytelling, but I wouldn't free her from our knot. That small act of defiance went a long way when it came time for me to explain the hoarding and the lapse in judgment on the couch purchase.

"I was just about to put my dinner in the oven," my mother said directly to Maezie, me having been reduced to some sort of accessory status between those new fast friends. "Have you two eaten already? Will you stay for dinner?"

Normally, I'd have jumped in right there because I knew what Saturday night at the Church house meant in terms of dinner, but I was too busy basking in the sound of "you two"—the way it had already been adopted into my mother's vernacular as a ready pronoun for her only son. Maezie wanted to stay, so she spoke up for the collective now known as "you two."

"Absolutely! Can I help you with anything?"

"No, but we need to hurry. *The Love Boat* comes on at eight."

And just like that, the two of them made for the central kitchen, leaving me mysteriously free and full of wonder at how either had negotiated their departure from the room without proper forethought. I did, however, receive a backward glance from my Maezie, a wink, and a blown kiss to keep my inner fire burning until her return. I smiled big, then replayed my mother's words yet again.

I could hear them laughing from the kitchen when I reached down and extracted the latest *Sharper Image* catalog from the top of the nearest pile. Good, I thought to myself, noting the cover was free of scribbled page numbers. I was the first to handle it and had a decent chance I could read it and put it back before my mother sensed its absence or remonstrated me for placing it out of order. Then I remembered what night it was and rushed to the kitchen, carelessly abandoning the catalog to the sandpaper clutches of the couch.

I slid two feet toward Rumpole the cat on an already ripped *Burpee* seed catalog from the previous spring, and he took off with a screech for the safety of the underside of my mother's bed. I righted myself somewhere along the back hall but was too late. The freezer door was wide ass open.

"Oh, good," my mother exclaimed with genuine pleasure. "I thought I had a couple more. I keep a few on hand in case Kenzie might show up."

Maezie had already been briefed. She knew. How much explaining can one guy do in an evening? I was going to have to pull over somewhere because there was no longer sufficient time to explain all I had on my plate. Speaking of plates...

"I just love these Hungry Hombre TV dinners!" my mother effused. "The Mexican cornbread is especially good."

I didn't hear the rest of the Supreme Madré's decree, not because I tuned her out but because Maezie pulled me close and kissed my cheek and her words sang to me, I promise you, when she offered me a trademark smile and said, "Beats the cafeteria, huh, babe?!"

You know, she had a valid point. I relaxed and time stood still while I surveyed the room and committed to memory the unlikely moment of happiness we three had stumbled upon. There was no denying the Supreme Madré, unique and precious in her own right, had come across to Maezie as the good and kind woman I knew her to be, and my gal had been received by the parent I wanted to most please that evening with equal appreciation.

And the cornbread did, in fact, kick some serious ass.

15

Judd

I don't recall exactly where on the planet the Supreme Madré went on her semiannual trip that winter but strongly suspect it was back to England. She and my father both had a passion for theater and enjoyed catching plays in London, albeit on different solo trips across the pond.

Madré had a tour guide she'd come to know on a series of packaged tours of the UK, and this trip was just another in that series, I suppose. All I distinctly remember was that Judd would be home alone when I finally brought Maezie out to meet him.

It was a Friday night and cold enough for a fire in the fireplace, which was our real motive for the visit to Pepper Ridge. Judd had never offered me any positive intel on dating, and certainly not marriage, so I neither sought nor cared what he thought of Maezie, but she needed to get a feel for him the way I had come to know Hugh so that she'd have a reference point in our future conversations or any historical tales I might share. Plus, as Scoon Penn noted, Maezie was Top Five on campus and Numero Uno in my heart, so I wanted to rub the old man's face in it. She could hold her own in his volleys of the King's English too—so dang smart—and she could and would make him laugh if he took the time to listen and absorb her persona.

It was a little after eight when we pulled into the driveway. Judd's Daimler was not in its usual spot, so I assumed he was still at the Hayride, supervising the Friday night dance and enjoying the break from routine brought about by Madré's two-week excursion. All the better for us lovebirds.

We crossed the house and passed through the paneled central kitchen enroute to "The Old Den" that was now a library/game room of sorts with shelves of books, a bumper pool table, and a large, comfortable couch fronting a corner fireplace. Maezie peeled off her rabbit coat and placed it on the breakfast table along with her purse before asking me rather matter-of-factly if I cared to join her in a Hungry Hombre TV dinner. She held her poker face far longer than I ever could while I seriously considered the merits of the Mexican cornbread. A playful yet forceful shove toward the den was the only indicator she'd been kidding, at least until that beautiful smile pushed her eyes into the crescents I simply adored. I set about stacking logs and preparing a glorious fire for this angel I was so proud of—this woman I was anxious to show off and present as "my better half."

"Hurry up!" Maezie scolded me as I lit the gas jet and worked with all due haste to replace the fireplace screen and take my seat beside her. "Get over here!" she unnecessarily completed her directive as she tugged me to her.

Any concept you may have of a romantic evening in front of a roaring fireplace was easily realized by us as we intertwined our arms and legs and watched the flames dance in each other's irises for untold minutes.

"What do you want to be when you grow up?" Maezie finally lobbed into the sacred silence.

I smiled and pretended to give the topic serious consideration for a good five or ten seconds.

"That's a pretty loaded question," I replied, buying me a little more time to search for a proper response.

"How so?"

"It assumes I have both the ability and desire to do so," I batted back. "Grow up, that is."

"True," Maezie countered flatly, leaving arched eyebrows as the only remaining clue she actually expected me to finish answering the question.

"No one has asked me that since I don't know when," I eked out in all sincerity. "Maybe never. Fleming & Burns is in my future whether I want it to be or not."

"That's why I asked what you wanted to be, not what you were going to do, Kenzie. Who are you? Who's in there?" was followed by a tapping on my chest.

I squirreled up my face, attempting some serious thought, but Maezie put a stop to that in a hurry. Her hand flew from my chest to my temple.

"Not there. Not that empty cavern," she offered as a smile spread across her face like wildfire. "Here," she emphasized, fingers back drumming on my breastbone and her eyes once more firing off semaphore signals as they searched mine in anticipation of my response.

I was touched by the moment and committed it to memory, and it stands the test of time to this day. I found myself suddenly emotional as I reached for the hand upon my chest and kissed each finger before allowing Maezie to stroke my cheek with it. Or was she wiping away a tear?

"I don't have a clue, Maezie," I said to my surprise.

She came to me in that frozen eon of time, so gentle and supporting, softly kissing each cheek then up to my eyelashes. This was an offering of pure love, a statement all at once comforting, and soothing...and brimming with confidence; something I had never experienced before.

I warmed to my core and allowed myself passage through some sort of veil and deep into my being, my emotions elevated to a plane somewhere above pure desire.

"Well, let's give it some thought, shall we?" the detached voice said as I fought to simply return to the present. "Where does your mama keep the Swiss Miss?"

"Kitchen," I managed along with a lame gesture that added "yonder" at best.

"Well, duh!"

And she departed to make us some hot chocolate. At last, the instant hot water tap would earn its keep beyond the chore of supplying my mother with quick and endless cups of Taster's Choice.

"You should be a comedy writer for *Letterman*. Or, better yet, you can take over for Johnny Carson," Maezie fantasized as she handed me my mug and took her place beside me on the couch. I must've made a face because she quickly followed with the cutest, "Whaaat?"

"Johnny Carson is an icon. I don't even know how they're gonna replace him if he ever retires," I commented.

"You're funny and a great writer. You come up with stuff that's way funnier than most of that crap. All the time."

"Okay, so how's that gonna work if we live in Colorado?"

"Fly in, tape a bunch of shows, then fly home."

"You've got this all figured out, don't you? What, may I ask, do you plan to do?"

"You mean, what do I want to be?"

"You left off the 'when I grow up' part."

"That was intentional. I don't plan on aging any further."

"*Now* you're with me."

Maezie was sipping hot chocolate when I smiled that last comment at her, eyes locked on mine. So angelic.

"I'm always with you, Kenzie, and always want to be, wherever that happens. Just so we're together. I'll be a gardener, and you can be a...butterfly rancher for all I care. Just so you're happy...*we're* happy."

There's a special feeling induced in the body when fangs of hot, brown liquid shoot out your nose rather than continue their journey to your stomach. As I imagined the demands of butterfly ranching, my laugh turned into some sort of "ack-ack" reminiscent of a cat in the throes of battling a furball.

"Oh, that's pleasant," I muttered, reaching for an already damp cocktail napkin in my saucer.

I focused on trying to abate the sneeze I knew would surely follow that ticklish assault, and Maezie became lost in a moment of Scoon Penn silent laughter.

"For better or worse. Those are the terms," I reminded her. "Best get used to it."

"Oh, god," she eventually responded as she dabbed at her moist eyes and worked to regain her composure.

The soggy napkin had barely cleared my septum when Maezie took my face in her hands and planted a wonderful kiss atop my stinging lips.

"For better or worse," she echoed.

An hour fell off the clock and neither of us noticed or cared in the slightest. Our world had no use for the markings of time.

Judd Church had several "tells" as the gambling world calls them, several signs that indicated his presence or approach to those trained to listen for them. Key among them were the shuffle of his well-worn house shoes that he virtually lived in around the clock, and his trademark cough from many years as an avid smoker.

I heard both emanating from the back hall and nodded to Maezie. *Show time.*

We stood and walked toward the common ground of the kitchen, hand in hand. Well, maybe I was tugging her a little, but we were unified in our approach.

"I.B.," my father called out in that rich radio voice of his when he shuffled into view.

"I.B." was Judd shorthand for "Idiot Boy," a name he blessed me with sometime in my youth, an alleged term of endearment (although I'm not exactly sure how) that stuck through the course of his lifetime. Remind me at some point to share the story of the time Judd introduced my mother and me to President Nixon as "my first wife, Loraine, and my idiot son, Kenzie." Oh, yeah, he really went there.

As my father rounded the corner to greet us, I was hell-bent on memorizing his initial reaction to my impeccably dressed, perfectly coiffed, *fucking stunning* girlfriend.

Oh, dear reader, I tell you, on seeing my lady, the moment slowed to molasses.

His pupils dilated like those of an addict receiving a stronger-than-expected dose of their drug of choice. Eyes darted from me to Maezie, briefly down her torso and back to her frozen smile, then a self-conscious glance at his own form clad in his favorite painter's pants and white, V-neck t-shirt so recently hidden under his stage costume. Not exactly what one would expect from the owner of Fleming & Burns nor from a master of any ceremonies. Judd Church mastered nothing in the remaining fraction of that second except the look of someone completely dumbfounded. I would never again see that expression grace his fallen face or witness an unfilled silence of any comparison.

Maezie broke Judd from this state with a steady "hello" that carried a little huskiness reminiscent of Suzanne Pleshette and delivered with just the right amount of charm and allure.

"Judd, this is Maezie," I said as if by rote, refusing to take my eyes from the face of my father as drama and awe danced about his features.

It seems weird to me when kids of any age call their parents by their first names. In my mind, they are forever "Mom, Dad, Mama, Papa" or such, but I'd taken to calling my father Judd as a swipe at his new stage personae, and the continued mocking felt right from that point on. To his credit, Judd recovered his place as father figure in the drama unfolding in the main kitchen and turned on the charm.

"Hello, my dear," he offered in accompaniment of a near lunge toward my girlfriend. Judd sandwiched Maezie's hand between his own and did his best to convey some level of sincerity as he tried to determine what she may or may not know about him.

Enough was what I saw in Maezie's eyes before they joined a heartwarming smile.

"So pleased to finally meet you," she said. And I believe maybe she was.

Judd could be a charmer when he wanted to be, and I sensed he wanted to be pretty damn charming right about then.

The next few minutes passed in small talk between them. Time caught up with our visit and just enough was exchanged between those two to satisfy the criteria of a thorough and complete first encounter without edging through to awkwardness. Maezie and I retreated toward The Old Den as the banter wound down, leaving Judd to the task of assembling a snack of Havarti cheese and Melba toast with a side of pepper jelly. He almost nodded at me when I reached back to pull the door closed, but that father-son moment could never launch from such an impromptu setting. In my well-documented naivety, I failed to grasp the threat Maezie presented to the Church empire in the mind of its current patriarch. Had I known, then the parting look Judd offered me would've been easily explained.

• • •

"The sun's up, Maezie."

You'd have thought I'd set fire to the fuse of a bomb. Maezie was at once upright and searching the room to get her bearings. I had some sort of Woody Woodpecker thing going on with my hair that relaxed her into laughter at my expense. We stood and stretched and looked upon the sad fire, now only a sputter of charred ends, yearning once more for the crackling splendor of last night's performance.

"Oh, shit! What about your dad?" Maezie blurted out.

My mind completed her thoughts.

"We didn't do nothin'," I replied, then continued once I received the *that's not the point* look from Maezie. "He won't leave for the Hayride for a couple more hours. We'll go out the side door, and he'll never be the wiser."

It was a good plan. Short lived, but good. The cold outside air jolted us both.

"My coat," Maezie said.

"I'll get it," my gentlemanly nature self-assured her. And there it was, mostly where she'd left it on the breakfast table. I grabbed it and her purse, taking note of the near empty cereal bowl that had displaced the pair.

"Never be the wiser," I heard Maezie share in a mocking tone from somewhere over my shoulder.

16

Heaven

I was sipping on a large frozen granita made with Café Lissadale "Private Reserve," courtesy of my man Quito, as I strolled along the M1 toward the business district of Manta—loving life, proud to be doing something productive after my hazy start to the day, and glad for the distraction from the excitement of my pending reunion with Maezie Fock. My destination was the Mall del Pacifico, more specifically, the MegaMaxi grocery store located just inside it.

Who was I kidding? The afternoon errand was no distraction. I was on a mission to procure all the necessary fixings for the reunion dinner I was planning to cook for the love of my life because a) she'd always loved my cooking, and b) I had something I wanted to make up to her.

• • •

It all started, oddly enough, while we were watching the *Newlywed Game* with the Supreme Madré, this time on a Friday night.

Announcer Johnny Gilbert was regaling the audience with details from the winning couple's prize package, which was to include a weeklong vacation to "beautiful Puerto Vallarta, Mexico!" The couple squealed with delight, hugging and bouncing and losing every one of the answer cards in the woman's lap. I shot a glance over to Maezie and, sure enough, she was sharing in the moment. I was certain she was visualizing us in the role of the happy couple while also dreaming of a similar trip out of the country. Right then and there, I made up my mind the time had come for me to make at least part of that dream come true.

Newlyweds? Not just yet, but we could damn sure act like it and take a trip somewhere.

The thought of seeing the larger world with Maezie sent chills all over my body, double chills when I felt her pump my hand because we always knew what the other one was thinking, and I found her smiling with a certain excitement I hadn't seen before. Just a "you two" thing, I guess, like growing up twinsies, I could only suppose.

We told the Supreme One we were headed to a movie when we bailed from Pea Ridge not long after, but the simple truth was both Maezie and I had reached our limit, not of my mother or the burlap couch I now regarded as a loveseat, but of our ability to contain our excitement for the trip that needed discussing and planning and researching.

My mother saw us to the door, and we weren't four steps toward my car before we heard the chain lock slide into place and were cast into darkness, either because my mother was ready to be rid of us and settle in with her latest Nero Wolfe mystery or, more likely, she was trying to afford us a little privacy.

Maezie and I hungered for one another. Our tumbling hearts had their own revolutions per minute, and we were both revved to redline levels when she took my face in her hands and made the first move toward some level of abatement. I perched her on the trunk of the car and tried to slow the pace while I fully absorbed and worked to understand the semaphore signals our eyes were flashing back and forth in their own beautifully soft and coded language. Maezie and I didn't need a romantic setting to explore our love because it could be counted upon to transform any location into our own private paradise.

We kissed until her eyelashes and their signals were all I desired, and I moved to press each one between my lips like one might save special flowers in the folds of a book, to be cherished and admired anew on other occasions. We merged into one another, and our ribs fit together, forming a stairway leading directly to our single beating heart. I didn't mind the hint of face powder that accompanied the salt coming from the moisture of either her eyes or mine as my lips began their journey back to hers, docking and undocking in heightened passion.

Our breathing unified, not in heaves of ecstasy but a relaxed weightlessness, an abandon found only at the hands of the most dedicated and experienced masseuse. Maezie knew how to work my heart, and time became a meaningless measurement, for who but a fool would ever want to know the end of what I was feeling.

Her earlobes deserved the nibbles I gave them, returning the favor from some eon passed that literally had my arm hair standing on end. Perfectly manicured nails, painted "strawberry" she told me, cradled my head like a proper easel, my face her willing canvas. Generations long gone would have called it "witchery." I knew only paradise. *Thistle* made an appearance as Maezie studied my face, planning the next stroke of what she considered a masterpiece.

"I love you," was the perfect accompaniment to the tennis match her eyes had just completed in their survey of mine. The softness of her words was like a cloud that swallowed me whole.

More tennis.

"I love you, too, my beautiful angel."

For she was. No other creature could have possibly conducted that tour of what I had no doubt was Heaven in every real and imagined sense of the word.

17

Polo Dirt

I was pulled back from my private reverie by a woman seeking better access to the blueberries that shared the display with the plump strawberries I'd been admiring inside the MegaMaxi grocery store for god only knows how long. That happens to me a lot these days. My mind drifts off into Maezieland at the slightest provocation or reminder of her. It could be a sight, a sound, a smell...and next thing I know, I'm stalled out, unable to continue in the modern world until my heart's had its fill of whatever particular memory my brain's shoved at it. I used to keep a tighter rein on shit like that. I came to and struggled to remember the way back to the hotel.

Once I got used to the idea that my marriage to Not Maezie was irrevocably headed to its conclusion, I expected to feel a general kind of all-over freedom. As you can imagine, I was genuinely surprised by the flood of Maezie-specific memories it offered up like some trove of mail held for a person who'd wandered home after being lost for decades. In this particular case, it was a tantalizing display of strawberries in a random grocery store in Ecuador that had triggered the pleasure ride back to my parents' darkened driveway.

Just a little bit longer and her hands would once more know their mates.

• • •

Announcer Johnny Gilbert had done one hell of a sales job on us. Maezie and I didn't even bother to consider any other place on the map and began planning our trip to "beautiful Puerto Vallarta, Mexico!" on the ride back to the dorm—although there wasn't a whole lot we could actually do, other than dream, until my mother's travel agent was in residence on Monday to arrange our bookings. Hopping up on the internet was still several more years in the future for most of us on the planet.

The lone window in my dorm room had already caused more harm to Maezie than I could tolerate, and she'd really worked hard to become Stan the RD's friend, but it was still pretty brazen when we abandoned that egress and began coming and going through the access door nearest my—*our*—suite at whatever time of night suited us with nary a thought for the consequences. We were given to laughter and Maezie's mirthful cadence floated around the dorm like some ambassador of femininity in open defiance of what was now fairly lax rules that were growing laxer by the minute. "As long as you stay under the radar and are cool about it," as Stan put it when no one else was around to hear him. Truth was, the sounds of femininity, in any form, were welcome in the all-male Cline dormitory at any hour on any day. For all intents and purposes, Maezie and I were now living together, and that made us both quite happy.

It was my left arm that started to go to sleep on the flight to Puerto Vallarta because I had arranged for Maezie to have the window seat for the journey down and back. Together, we discovered the wonder of Biscoff cookies on that flight, and it was all I could do to surrender the extras I'd pilfered from the drink cart when no one was looking. But, hey, small sacrifice for the woman I loved. Maezie, however, was generous in sharing the score, and I enjoyed being hand-fed an equitable amount as men far more macho than me took note of the pretty señorita with the amazing eyes doting on her "seatmate." Jealousy never once reared its head in our union, so secure were we with one another, so convinced our choices could not be improved upon, and so determined to honor each other for always.

I tell you, Jim Swann was simply the best travel agent on the planet. He was a longtime friend of the family, and my mother relied on him for all her world travels. I was the one that collected the reward for whatever strings Jim had pulled to score Maezie and me the Honeymoon Suite at the

Posada Vallarta, replete with our own private hot tub. The fact that all those newlyweds Bob Eubanks had sent to the city had ended up in that very room was not lost on us. We felt like celebrities, and she thought me the ultimate romantic.

We changed and were soon walking the beach, admiring the thatched huts scattered along Bahia de Banderas Bay that held all manner of boutiques and gift shops.

Maezie wasted no time selecting a stunning embroidered, off-the-shoulder dress piped in white lace for herself and a handsome Mexican wedding shirt in seafoam green for me. That night at dinner, we would play the part of newlyweds to the hilt, as if we needed any costuming or prompting to do so. The staff could assume whatever they wanted to and, who knows, it might even get us a glass or two of free champagne.

I made a reservation for 7:00 p.m. in the restaurant downstairs. The rest of the city could wait until we were a little more settled from our flight. A few minutes before the appointed hour, Maezie finished freshening up and presented herself in full Mexican attire before me.

"How do I look?" she bashfully inquired.

The contrast between the modest tan of her skin and the intricate lace of her sleeves was the first thing my eyes took note of as I struggled to emit the "wow" that eventually found its way quietly into the suite. Each colorful flower that encircled the bodice of that amazing dress was echoed by her choice of earrings or shoes or necklace...or her genuinely happy eyes. The central flower, over her heart, was the color of my shirt. We matched to perfection, and that was the start of a tradition we shared for the rest of our courtship and, hopefully, would share again once more.

As the only child of the owner of the largest men's store in the entire southern United States, I could've filled my closets back home with all manner of suits, but I was happy with just a few well-chosen ones. Ties, however, were another matter. My collection of cravats was on par with the shoe collection of Imelda Marcos. Not because I was a shopaholic, but because I was lazy in the morning times and didn't want to think about my tie selection, so I'd often go to work with an open collar and choose a fresh one from the rack. I figured $15 ties were a better indulgence than suits costing upward of $200, and General Manager Barbunzo appreciated my concern for the store's bottom line.

For church or a fancy night out, Maezie could always count on her man Kenzie to have in his possession the perfect tie to highlight whatever outfit she could dream up—and, oh, my gal knew how to dress herself and how to make an entrance. And one needed no further proof of that than to witness the flabbergasted quasi-groom on the receiving end of her query in the Honeymoon Suite that blissfully perfect night in Mexico.

If I knew the trade of a cobbler as I write these words, I could reconstruct for you the lipstick-red shoes Maezie concluded her outfit with that evening, so enamored of them I became. The heel that I can only truly and properly describe as "sexy" pushed her height to just over mine, offering me a fresh vantage point from which to admire the stylings of her hair, always matching the occasion to perfection. Her eye makeup shimmered as the green of my shirt rose above the eyeliner and gave way to silver highlights that turned smoky as they reached her perfectly defined eyebrows. Something, either the misty droplets of her hair spray or some actual hint of glitter made her hair sparkle with the newness of an exquisite tiara and made me wish in that moment I had the jewels of royalty to shower Maezie in forevermore.

I couldn't respond to her above a primal growl before she grabbed my arm and said, "We gotta go!"

And so, we did.

I was taken aback when the host ushered us to our table for two set against the center of the back wall behind a wonderfully rhythmic and soothing fountain that was to enhance the peaceful parade of romantic thoughts we both were having in the splendor of our surroundings. I shamelessly cut in front of our host so that I, and not he, had the pleasure of pulling out Maezie's chair—in this case a beautiful highbacked wicker throne exactly like the one Morticia ruled from on *The Addams Family*. (If you haven't noticed already, I loved that show.)

"Thank you, dahling!" Maezie said as she took her seat, fully aware we were sharing the same thought and playing off it so perfectly. I wanted to attack her arm in the spirit of Gomez Addams but instead made for my own wicker throne to await the snap and placement of the napkin upon the lap that our host had just presented Maezie with along with a rather tall, somewhat cumbersome embossed leather menu.

"We'll both have the *Pollo Chocolate*," I instructed the waiter a good fifteen relaxing minutes after he brought "the newlyweds" a glass of champagne, compliments of the house. Chocolate is always a happy thing, and we were both intrigued with its pairing with chicken, so Maezie and I offered our last sips in toast of the unique dish headed our way under silver domes right about the time we should be finishing the refills that had somehow materialized as soon as our glasses settled back upon the table. It wasn't clear if the refills were free as well, but then, not much was clear to us from that point on....

Watching Maezie make a face like a foo dog halfway through her first bite of *Pollo Chocolate* as she debated whether she should spit the contents of her mouth into her napkin or project it into the overwatered snake plant beside the table was an unwelcome indicator the night was trying to take a turn, and I simply wasn't going to stand for it. In a show of solidarity, I allowed the portion on my fork to continue its journey to my mouth as Maezie placed her hand on my free one and shook her head "no."

"*Polo Dirt Chocolate* is probably a better name," she remarked.

"Ugh," I said while contorting my face to match her foo dog expression. "Tastes like chocolate chalk! Must've used baker's chocolate."

"I'm sticking with *polo dirt*," Maezie said as she swished the last of the water in her glass like a kid trying to wash away the grit from the dentist's tooth powder. She spit it back into her empty glass, then contributed further to the demise of the snake plant with a smooth flick of her wrist.

"The asparagus is pretty good," I countered. "And so is the rice if you steer clear of the chocolate sauce."

"Trust me," Maezie came back. "I'm not even on the same road as that crap. Let's go upstairs and order room service," she brightened. "Maybe jump in the hot tub."

Suddenly, my stomach was full. Butterflies of pure joy. Maezie stroked the back of my hand and lightning shot up my arm.

"I mean, that is what honeymooners do, isn't it...dahling?"

The look! The white lace dress, the tan skin, those amazing red shoes, the sparkling hair, the smoky eyeshadow...all framed in the circle of her highbacked wicker throne was just too much perfection for any mortal man to stand.

"*Cara Mia*," I uttered on autopilot from my trance. "Check, please!" followed as close behind as I could manage, offered to any servant within earshot, for I never took my eyes off my Maezie the rest of the evening.

The balance of the trip, I will allow, was pure magic. We saw things, bought things, learned things, shared things, and discovered more things we had in common.

And we fell deeper in love.

18

Chicken Pontalba

I think it is time, dear reader, for a course correction of sorts.

"You got married on that trip, didn't you?" I can hear you wanting to ask. "So perfect, so in love. So meant to be."

Maezie and I were madly in love. There is absolutely no denying that fact, but the maturity and insight of the words I offer you in this journal, the "wisdom born of pain" Helen Reddy spoke of in her song, must factor into this tale at some point because Maezie and Kenzie didn't have all the answers back then. I'm not sure we do now, but at least we've collected enough "been there, done that" experiences to share a collective wisdom and the courage to believe our convictions as we finally steer ourselves together once more.

Maezie Fock is back in my life, and I am never letting her go again.

I don't know that I need to proselytize, pontificate, preach, or pander that point further, for I imagine you have a story of your own, some tale where a significant other hijacked your thoughts, your heart, and your life altogether. However, in case you don't...

Picture a 1960s era farm truck, restored just enough to appear more than a junker but still in need of a little spit and polish. It runs great and looks cool in that comfortably worn favorite chair kind of way. This is your daily driver. You know it inside and out, and you can rely on it. The problems, the nicks and tears, you know them all. This is your baby.

The stereo works but the '70s era JBLs need replacing. The left speaker hasn't worked since the '90s, and you've been meaning to fix it, but have gotten used to the one, and it's no big deal. I mean, before earbuds and headphones, we just had a single earpiece anyway. You've made do.

Then, all of a sudden, you're driving down the road, jamming out to Sammy Hagar singing that he can't drive 55 (and you proudly note the truck is pushing 60), and that left speaker comes back into play, and you almost wreck.

"Holy shit!" you marvel, and rightfully so because the music is now totally different—driven and delivered with passion and sounding so damn awesome! You drive on like someone possessed, singing loudly to the music and in your own little world. Yesteryear has come to life again. When the song ends, you get out of the truck, take a rag and some compound, and the finish comes right back. The truck looks amazing, you feel amazing, and in the span of "I Can't Drive 55," your entire outlook has been altered and will never be the same.

• • •

Maezie Fock came back into my life a few months ago, bringing with her some fix for that second speaker, and this is where you can relate, I know you can. Maezie altered the DNA of my life, and all I could do was wonder what in the hell I had going on during all our years apart...that kept us apart. The music in my truck sounded richer, the food I was eating tasted fresher, the bills I had to pay were more reasonable...I mean, take your pick. Work wasn't the pain it usually was, phone calls about extended car warranties could be tolerated to the point that I just wanted to run out in the street—flagging down anyone professing any sort of interest in what this mad man was up to—and shout, "Look at my world! Look at what has changed! You, too, can experience this!"

I entered a different orbit the day that speaker came back to life. I hadn't noticed its gradual decline and had come to tolerate its absence but hearing it once more...I would never live that way again. I don't know what I was thinking.

People have affected you that way, haven't they? You've been consumed by someone, haven't you? You've been that old truck in need of some sprucing up and have had your world taken over by love. Or have you?

This book has been an assemblage of many great stories from my shared history with Maezie. I cherry-picked the good stuff and strung it together, not to obscure the pain and the downside, but to shine a light on the beautiful, neglected elements of life that too often don't get their proper time in the spotlight. My point: Maezie and I experienced every one of these professed stories, and we were aware of the love we'd crafted, but we had our lessons to learn as well. We made mistakes, just like anybody else. But we got way more right than wrong, and the core of this story remains one of blinding love.

I've read my words in this journal and disappeared into bliss at my recollections of the past, but I will tell you here and now that when the left JBL came back on in my truck, and I had the age and wisdom and gratitude to appreciate what that meant, I had no way on earth to convey all the wonder and joy and amazement I felt for my Maezie Fock.

Still don't.

Maybe it was like when moviegoers in 1939 saw *The Wizard of Oz* explode from black and white into full blown color for the first time. No, it was more than that. The speaker moment eclipsed any I've written about to this point.

And we are nowhere near the summit.

I've been given a chance to shine anew and have discovered, in the process, that Maezie and I were right about each other, and right for each other, all along. She and I have glimpsed steps leading higher still, the path we knew in our hearts was there but could never pin down, and I couldn't wait to take her hand for the continued ascent.

Now, on to Chicken Pontalba.

• • •

I found what I needed on my trip to the MegaMaxi grocery store, despite my stall out in front of the strawberries. I'd been daydreaming of our reunion in every possible setting, from every possible camera angle, playing every possible background song, and so forth, and I got so excited that I didn't know what to do. I found myself committed to erasing the memory of *Polo Dirt Chocolate* with a slam-dunk presentation of New Orleans cooking at its finest—my interpretation of the classic dish known as Chicken Pontalba. Yes, I'd conscripted myself to cook for Maezie Fock in the days ahead. No, I didn't think my stomach would allow me to eat any of it if I couldn't get the butterflies currently in residence to move on.

The dish, which many New Orleans locals consider one of the finest ever conceived, was created at the legendary Brennan's Restaurant in the French Quarter by Chef Paul Blange in the early 1950s, and named for Baroness Micaela Pontalba who, legend has it, was a beautiful social maven noted for her lavish parties and rich creole dishes. Featuring mushrooms, garlic, ham, potatoes, and other yummies and topped with a bearnaise sauce. Perfection or, in other words, as far removed from chocolate chalk chicken as you can possibly get.

New Orleans has been my home for going on ten years. Homer Fleming's bride, Julia, known to descendants as "Mama Julia," hailed from the city. Her grandfather, Philippe, a third-generation watchmaker, emigrated to New Orleans in 1839 from Switzerland and died in a yellow fever outbreak just seven years later. "Bourquin" was the family name. French, to be sure, but not descendants of the Acadian French who migrated down from Nova Scotia and settled in the swamps of Louisiana to fish and prosper as "Cajuns." Still, the Bourquins knew their way around the kitchen and their heritage served to further inspire the selection of Chicken Pontalba for my precious Maezie.

As I made my way to the Hotel Vistalmar's back patio—my mind busy calculating the odds of all those groceries actually fitting in the tiny fridge in my room—the surrounding speakers blasted a Tim McGraw song that spoke my heart, my yearning, my resolve and dedication in that moment.

"Just to See You Smile."

"How is it possible to love someone so much?" I wondered as the clouds turned purple and pink and blended into the image of Maezie's gorgeous smiling face in my mind's eye.

I felt like the luckiest man alive.

19
Prescience

I am not coming. Now, please forget me and move on.

Two sentences. One feeble text—who knew the context from which it was sent, but in an instant, the Universe had turned my whole world upside down.

Seriously? was all I could manage as a reply.

More than serious. I am married. Please let me be.

What happened? I typed but ended up erasing it because I knew the answer.

There was no way I could hate this woman or her decision *and* love her for her values at the same time. I thought if I offered her the place she longed to retire to—Ecuador, made something of myself, lost weight, tried to rewind the clock, pointed out the obvious...

The shoe was now on the other foot, and it hurt like hell. Maezie was stuck in Marriage #3, a prisoner of her commitment to the institution, and there was nothing more I could say or do—*should* say or do—to facilitate its inevitable destruction. Maezie isn't the kind of person who gives up. She loves the way I long to be loved again. She is an unshakeable partner. I knew better than to take her to this point, but I couldn't help myself. *You push, and people fall and get hurt.* It really is that simple. Selfish. Stupid.

That has been our battle over the last year, excited to reconnect but quickly realizing a simple friendship was out of the question, so then what? I tried to keep the texts and emails to a minimum, knowing it wasn't fair of me to stand in the shadows, tapping my foot like some metronome Maezie was coerced to keep up with, some maddening sound that forces a choice that someone of her principles should never have to make. The resulting bomb came as no real surprise.

I tried to tell you "off limits" from the start, but you wouldn't listen.

Yes, and you also told me "You have me. My heart." I thought to myself but didn't send that reply. Maezie was hurt and angry, and I couldn't blame her. I'd selfishly pursued my own agenda, leaving her to figure out how to end her destructive marriage in some sort of honorable way, while my fingers were wrapped securely around the crowbar wedged in the middle of her life, waiting for the word "go."

Not even ten months ago, the exchange was so very different....

You loved me. You love me still. I am the same. I was convinced at one point you hated me.

Never. I stalked you from afar. Well, mostly afar.

I'm laughing now!

My muscles tensed. I was, all at once, embarrassed to be here, in Ecuador, embarrassed of the whole orchestration, and angry at myself for trying to bend the Universe to my will.

Miske, the elixir damned to be my only companion, appeared in my thoughts and offered a way out of my misery. I summoned Quito and requested an entire bottle.

You know I can't do anything but love you from afar? You and he are the same people. Guess I was looking for you?

20

Comfort on a Bed of Nails

I was in pursuit of the complex task of clearing my mind, assisted by the dwindling contents of the miske bottle, which challenged the delivery of the beauty that still remained in my swooning head.

I want to count her perfect teeth with my tongue.
I want to memorize and delight in where time has taken her body.
I want to settle atop the scar she showed me in that private place.
Home.

I want to dance fearless before her beautiful mind,
Say anything, like now, because she knows my soul.
And that is so fucking exhilarating.

I want to sell all this surplus energy back to her grid.
Spend it like a crazy woman. Just keep it coming.
So much at hand now. So wild and unregulated.
But someone's got to pay for this, I keep thinking.

We share the needle, but sharing is good, right?

She wants to read every word I've ever written
Because they all praise her in some fashion.
And that feels good.
She wants to jump because we've always had fun
But knows you could crush a person from that height
If they were to stumble underneath.

She wants to get it "right."
Always has done so. Always will.
How quiet that word can be sometimes.
How cruel that she is made my reliable regulator
And I, her faithful test of time.

I want her to put on the record of her life
And turn it up loud as shit
To my memory every last tragic crash and every beautiful note
So that I may marvel in the orchestra leader and massage her tired shoulders

And we may come to know how to make softer sounds together
And make us grateful we will always have each other.

What price salvation now?
I don't care. Just write the fucking check.
Let us live as we die and die as we live.
Just, please, together.
Best friends at least.
Inextricably intertwined.
Because there is such comfort found on our bed of nails.

Quito took the pen from my hand, closed the cover of my journal, and quietly took my glass with a sad smile.

21

A Broken Record

"You're too good for your own good," Maezie told me more than once during our college days, and she repeated that mantra in recent months, more as a warning as my one and only attempt at a marriage sputtered to its conclusion. Fair enough. I tended to put myself last, ever hopeful people would treat me on par with how I treated them, but such was rarely the case.

"You know, I hold you responsible for setting the bar so high," I told her in my defense. "Everyone since has failed to measure up."

"I'm talking about people in general," she lectured me. "You and I are so much alike, giving all we've got until we're used up. I don't know about you, but I'm tired...tired of the whole deal."

• • •

I've come to know there's a word for that, for us, for the condition that has mutually afflicted Maezie and me in all those years we've spent apart: *empath*.

The all-too-handy online sources define an *empath* as "a person with the paranormal ability to apprehend the mental or emotional state of another individual." They also suggest the word is used chiefly in science fiction, which I can accept, as the concept and the affliction has always felt otherworldly. An empath is a person who absorbs other people's emotions in a genuine sense. When an empath says, "I feel your pain," they truly do, and go out of their way to help alleviate it. Empath is the obvious root of the more familiar word *empathy*, which indicates a person's ability to put themselves in the shoes of another. The trouble with empaths is we tend to leave the shoes on until a pair of the next wounded person is left on our *Welcome* mat, forgetting in the process what has become of our own worn-out footwear.

How's it going down there? inquired my good friend, Robbie, via text as I brushed my teeth in preparation for another ill-planned round of drinking. *I'm dying to know.*

I'm just dying, I replied. *Maezie's not coming.*

A *ping* from my phone indicated Robbie had more to say on the subject, but I didn't.

"Stir the ashes and drown again," I heard my scoutmaster or Smokey the Bear say as I yanked open the door to my sad, little room and felt the setting sun dissolve my bloodshot eyes.

"I feel like I've drowned," I sang in tribute to the recently departed Jimmy Buffett who was, once more, my hero. "Margaritaville, here I come."

22

The Fourth Step

Over forty? Obviously. Victim of fate? Maybe. Too late?

I don't want to talk about it. Buffet had definitely overstayed his welcome, and I was pushing mine with another visit to the patio. I'd thought another of Quito's amazing frozen margaritas would do the trick as I'd always viewed being wasted away in Margaritaville as the best relief one could possibly find if they ever found themselves in my situation. But it wasn't working, and I didn't appreciate Jimmy occupying space in my head that should've been dedicated to grieving.

Enjoy Heaven, Parrot Head, and leave me be.

• • •

My mother spent her sixtieth birthday in rehab. And I put her there.

Judd was cavorting around London on his annual solo outing, so the responsibility was all mine. The Supreme Madré could go years without touching alcohol, but if Judd ever left town for more than a day or two, she'd get hammered and stay that way, always careful to stop a few days before his return. The combo of alcohol and some new medication put her in the yard that morning, ranting at me about all my biker friends—partying in the attic—that had to go home. When she told me I needed to "go pack a suitcase for our trip to Scotland," where she was going to finally receive a new body, I decided something had to be done.

I called a former roommate, "Moss," for advice. His name was Danny, but I called him Moss because he couldn't grow a beard for shit. His dad was some honcho with the Council on Alcoholism & Drug Abuse, so I figured he'd know what to do. He did, and the Supreme One was admitted to Clearwood Forest by Yours Truly later that day. Madré thought we were going to the airport. I slithered out of the rehab facility as day turned to night, feeling like I'd betrayed my sweet mama on some deep level.

• • •

I didn't inherit my mother's predisposition to alcohol, so my margarita binge had nothing to do with the ugly memory that floated to the surface at that particular moment. I was simply trying to change channels in my brain. Truth be known, the margarita was just something to sip on until the THC gummies kicked in. Yes, *gummies*. Plural.

"I don't often choose cannabis products for relief," I heard the voice in my head paraphrase the guy from the beer commercial, "but when I do, it's because I really need them."

The memory of Madré's miserable sixtieth was fighting for pole position despite my having been fully exonerated three days later when I visited her, and she told me I'd saved her life. My brain was trying to lead off the examination of my every shortcoming, and I was simply rolling over.

It was at the codependency group therapy I was made to attend as part of Madré's recovery where I'd first become aware that we "don't always see ourselves as others do." Some chick I didn't know and wouldn't otherwise have tried to know, called bullshit on whatever posturing I was up to in that session, and I started to get mad. But something told me there was value in what she was saying because no one was paying her to say it, and she wasn't out to hurt me for no reason. I took my lumps but managed a snipe or two at her before the session was over, or at least my jumbled cranium remembered it that way.

I am devolving.

Yes, I have shortcomings, a multitude of them, but because of that one session, I've developed a keen awareness and willingness to at least consider the opinions of others. That, and the fact that I'm a return-the-shopping-cart kinda guy, should've counted for something.

I took another sip of my margarita and, after suffering immense pain in the upper part of my throat—a fucking brain freeze—I took another sip, because I stupidly believed the cold had anesthetized the area in question. Wrong! My only hope for the day was to ride my buzz the hell away from there.

Who knows what time it was when I managed to find a dark place to hide on the beach at some point, dragging a lounge chair into the middle of some big, bushy palm plant thingy. All I recall was it was an amazingly starry night and bugs were busy gnawing on me, and I didn't give a shit. I wasn't far from the mall, but the light pollution was minimal from the makeshift fort of mine.

It doesn't matter if I drink to excess or smoke a bunch of pot or chew a handful of gummies, I'm destined to pass out fast asleep, and that's pretty much what happened as far as I can tell.

Tonight, my eyes were reluctant to open, but my brain was ready to resume the tennis match I'd skipped out on with Robbie.

"So...you wanna start or shall I?" my motherfuckin' gray matter lobbed onto the court of darkness. I didn't say a word. "Step Four is a biggie, my man. A fearless moral inventory of ourselves."

"I'm not up for it."

"Didn't ask if you were. Don't care. You're the one driving this bus to Hell, Kenzie. I'm just along for the ride."

And that was the discussion I'd had with my brain either in my room or at the bar or in my dark place or come to think of it...all of the above.

One moral inventory coming up. Eventually.
Cue the tears.

23

Cannonball

I was fucked up! Those THC gummies put me down for a nap who knew when, and I promise you, I made a sincere effort to vacate my palm fort at some point, but *damn!* The stars were really out, and the breeze felt good. The gummies arrived in all their glory, motioning me aboard for a quick cannonball ride to oblivion. I didn't resist.

As my mind wandered, I was determined to wrestle control of the narrative in my head. Wasn't sure if that was possible or if I could maintain focus for more than a few seconds, but I felt loose enough to give it a try.

• • •

Maezie's perfume was something of gardenias—*White Shoulders, Soft Shoulders, Bare Shoulders...Flowerpot #9, something.*

She's told me before, but that trivia was far from my mind. Blissful sensory overload was all I knew. *White Shoulders*, my mind resolved as my mouth moved toward her *bare shoulders*. Win-win.

Deborah Harry was singing in my head about rolling around in designer sheets when I bought the Monsanto king-sized bed set, complete with comforter, sham, and all those damn pillows, and she was singing now as my fantasy was about to be realized.

My dorm room, like every other dorm room, came with two single beds but, since it was just *moi* in residence, I shoved them together to form a king. I wasn't the first to come up with that brilliant idea, but I was pretty sure I was the first to fill in the crack between the mattresses with that T-shaped foam thing Sears sold for just that purpose. And I was damn sure I was the first to pay whatever hundreds this cocoa-brown bedding ensemble set me back. Frickin' dorm room bedding.

Built upon a quilted mattress pad and then littered with those glorious sheets and all those pillows—the *Playground* was primo. That happened a week or so before I'd ever met Maezie.

Truth be told, Trini Brown was the inspiration for the choices I made on my shopping spree at Sears during the delusion that she and I would, at some point, be getting back together.

• • •

I laughed uncontrollably, fed by the humor I'd somehow found in the sacred memory of Maezie and our first night sleeping together or perhaps due to the fact I'd tried four times to leave my palm fort, and each time, my feet landed between the vinyl strands of the lounge chair, and careened me back into place.

Miss January. Yes, I actually said that while topless Trini was cinching her white linen drawstring pants and preparing to flee my life for good. *Yes, my memory can be painfully exacting, especially when my brain's in self-torture mode, which is often.* Yes, Trini rolled her eyes in response. Ask me why that memory bares itself anytime anyone rolls their eyes at me for any reason at all.

Miske, my feet tried to tell me with their progression back toward the Vista del Mar.

"No, no. Fuck you!" I lectured the cool night air. "I'm doing just fine, thankyouverymuch," I offered in a rebuttal to my compromised thought process.

And with that, my still-impressively-cute-for-a-middle-aged-guy ass plopped down in the sand, and the hypnotic sound of the surf was all I heard for the next minute, or an hour.

Wet. Forget all the other adjectives I mumbled earlier. My ass was *wet* from the encroaching surf. *Maybe I'll go have a beer.* Better idea than miske or another frozen margarita. I stood and brushed wet sand from my backside, then wiped my now wet-and-sandy hand on my knee until clumps of it stopped hitting my bare feet. "Hey, I'm wearing linen drawstring pants! I'll be goddamned! If I take off my shirt, reckon I can be Miss January?!" I cracked myself up.

• • •

"You're perfect for me. Maybe I shouldn't say this, but so help me, it's true. I don't know how, but it's true. I love you, Mackenzie."

I think our eyelashes touched. I meant to answer Maezie with the same thoughts and same certainty, but I was fascinated with the feeling in my heart and slightly concerned with the feeling in my stomach. So, this was what butterflies felt like. This was what love felt like. An aggressive kiss battled between us, satisfied to wait out the audible response from me that was coming. I always look at the pictures before I read the text, so this was pretty much the same thing, or not at all.

"You are the center of my universe, Maezie," I said without taking my eyes from hers, which was a first for me with pretty much anyone. "All I've ever wanted from life is emanating from you, right here, right now. I love you too. Of that, I am certain, but my words don't do my feelings justice. This...you..."

"I know, my love. I know."

She stroked my cheek and kissed my eyelashes as both our hands started to roam over what had become one glorious, single, and perfect union. There were times of hunger, many actually, but for that moment we harvested our love for one another one silken handful at a time. Gliding, caressing. Slowly, purposefully. There was a banquet of unknown splendor before us, and we aimed to take full advantage of it. Somewhere in the hours that followed, her back arched as mirthful moans became cries of ecstasy. We triumphed, and our souls moved in together.

In the morning, Maezie informed me that I hadn't snored. She described a purring sound, and then the hours slipped away once more with little more said between us.

Arches and ecstasy.

24

The Cart & the Horse

"Hey! Wake up!" my mind offered a little too loudly in the predawn hours of *Shitty Day: The Sequel.* "How 'bout that time Maezie came at your dad with a pitchfork?! That was some shit, wasn't it?! How'd it go again?"

The thing about me, most of the time anyway, is once I'm awake, I'm awake.

Having never made it to my next beverage, that beer, I unfolded myself from the fetal position atop a vinyl lounge chair and, this time, managed to exit the palm fort, my apparent place of refuge. In doing so, I drew the ire of an obviously European couple. I say *obviously* because why else would the pot-bellied (yet impressively tan) man of this set be sporting a banana hammock to walk the beach with his old lady before the sun had completed its entrance for the day?

Disrespect for God, perhaps? I decided, answering myself.

For her part, Mrs. Hammock looked like burnt toast, showcasing under boob, side boob, and plenty of standard above boob along with a camel toe that added new meaning to the term *crack of dawn*. Her darkened hide reminded me of the well-worn seats in my first BMW. She muttered foreign words I was sure were for me and "unkind" at best before favoring me with her retreating ass that, were it up to me, would've been awarded its own zip code.

I somehow made it back to my room. The sand-covered key turned the lock after several wipings and a few wishful prayers.

My beeline for the bathroom was interrupted by the appearance in the mirror of what looked like Kevin from *Home Alone* after he tried aftershave for the first time. And all I needed was some bleach for my hair and I'd have been a shoo-in for a cooking show host. I would've laughed, but I was fascinated with the pattern on my face from the vinyl slats that made it look like I'd lost a fight with a set of Venetian blinds. No wonder the Hammocks were horrified.

Does anyone still even say "Venetian blinds?" I wondered as my pollution of the already stale atmosphere of Room 5 began ahead of schedule. I closed the door to the toilet only briefly before I realized, once more, that I was alone. Now and forevermore. I flung it back open in an act of defiance.

"Let 'er rip, tater chip!" I declared to no one as I assumed the position.

"So, how'd it go again?" my indulgent mind wanted to know. This time, I acquiesced, but found a different story had been conjured by circumstance. *If my brain had its way, Maezie and the Pitchfork would have to wait.*

"No!" I shouted into the empty shell of Room 5 as I forced myself to concentrate on the image of Maezie advancing on my father with a pitchfork in her hand and a scowl reminiscent of a certain orange-skinned ex-President's mugshot. The story of the impeccably bad timing of a clogged toilet during one of my post-college reunions with Maezie was just too painful right then, albeit funny as hell, at least in retrospect. But I wasn't going there.

• • •

Judd was in mid-supervision of the body work on the '32 Plymouth that occupied the garage complex behind the house at Pepper Ridge on that particular steamy Friday in August of '81. "Have you lost your mind?!" he bellowed.

Rod and Bruce froze in place to see if their boss was directing his venom at them. Judd had recently taken a fancy to car restoration in "semi-retirement" and had begun taking a few days off from his precious Hayride (and, of course, from Fleming & Burns) to oversee the work of the displaced Wisconsin duo who knew their way around classic cars far better than he. No, Judd's wrath was reserved solely for Yours Truly.

It was not the reaction I'd anticipated when I flashed Mama Julia's wedding ring and informed him I was going to ask Liesel Almay Fock to marry me that very evening.

"Son, no. Think this through," Judd continued, oblivious that his words were destroying the tentative bond we'd begun to forge of late through my contributions to his car projects.

I liked painting the metal dash to look like burled walnut, and I was getting pretty good at glass etching and thought the crossed roses on the oval rear window looked nothing short of *bitchin'*. I even took an auto shop class the previous summer to learn my way around engines. There had always been and would always be nothing I wouldn't do to win my father's approval.

In this moment, however, I hated the motherfucker, and it was only the sense of proper decorum I was raised with that kept me standing there listening as he kept right on with Speech 23, a selection he'd no doubt been expecting to have to call into service sooner rather than later.

"You're just starting out in life," he droned on. "There'll be plenty of time to think about that later. Trust me, there's money in it for you if you just wait, and more money if you never marry at all."

Forty-plus years later, I still have no idea what the hell that last sentence was ever supposed to mean. It wasn't a bribe (I don't think). The best I could come up with was that Judd was advising me from his perch atop his own failed marriage that if you don't take on a partner right away, you can keep all your earnings and build an empire quicker. And—point number two—if you stay a bachelor, you'll never have to share with anyone ever and live like a king. A lonely ass king. Spoken by a man who had no concept *at all* of the love his son had come to know through sheer determination despite the negative example set by his pappy.

"A good woman is like a trolley. Another one will come along in a few minutes. There's no reason for you to cast your lot with the first floozy that gives you the time of day."

Trolley? Floozy? This decade, please!

"Floozy?!" I reacted. "Where's that coming from? Maezie's a wonderful girl. You only met her once in the past year!"

"And that's all it took," he huffed. "Sleeping with you on the first date," he muttered. "Don't let her fool you, Mackenzie. She's after one thing only."

"First of all, it wasn't our first date, more like our thirtieth, but you wouldn't know that because you're pouring yourself into everyone's life but mine and only care about the parts of my life that fit into your plan for my future. Second of all, we fell asleep on the couch that night, if you must know, and Maezie was mortified. I told her it was no big deal. Boy, was I wrong."

Judd had stepped in his own shit and had nowhere to go. As I studied his fallen face, it was the first time I recalled actually feeling sorry for the man who, up to that morning, I would've done anything to emulate.

I was livid and just turned and walked out of the shop. The Supreme Madré was watering in the backyard and, despite the anger on my face, asked me how it went with Judd. Somewhere in the opening seconds of my rant, my hands flew skyward in emphasis and the ring I'd been pridefully showcasing went flying into the lush St. Augustine grass. Anger turned to panic as my mother quickly joined me in the search for Mama Julia's family heirloom.

Forty-five minutes later, after a group effort involving Team Rod & Bruce, I found the ring among the cannas and received what I will forever recall as the greatest hug ever from my sainted mother along with the sweetest reassurance and well wishes.

"Dat sure is a pretty ring, dere," Bruce said in his extreme Wisconsin accent, and this time I didn't find it the least bit annoying. "You best go find your lady and put it on her before something else happens," he kidded me.

"Yeah, you've got that right, Bruce," I offered along with a handshake. "I appreciate you guys helping with the search."

It was now quitting time, and Judd slithered from the garage, casting a quick glance at the gathering of four in the backyard before making an extended show of locking up, so he wouldn't have to join the party he was not welcome to attend. I could only assume he was relieved when I made my exit through the breezeway and headed for Texas and the woman I intended to marry.

Oh, the beauty of that magic moment when I asked Maezie Fock to be my bride! She'd told me at the start of summer she might be expecting a ring soon, but the gal didn't see it coming when it finally happened as our one-year anniversary drew near.

Mama Julia's wedding ring was impressive, to say the least, a two carat Asscher cut diamond flanked with four baguette-cut diamonds and four single-cut diamonds underneath each side of the bridge, all in a platinum setting. It was clear and bright and gorgeous. Homer Fleming wasn't playing around back in the day and, fittingly, neither was I.

Let's just say I was the one relieved when I settled behind the wheel of the Riviera and pointed it toward Uncertain. I had close to an hour to rinse my mind free of the stain Judd had oozed upon it. I popped the *Hooked on Classics* tape into the player and let the music envelope me in beautiful sounds as I focused on the prize—Maezie, mine for all to see, mine forever.

In recent weeks, in addition to running up a ridiculous phone bill of over $400 in long distance calls to my beloved, I'd begun "priming the pump," so to speak, with little gifts in the mail. Nothing fancy, earrings and such, to let my Maezie know we were going to survive the summer just fine and grow even closer.

"I know that no one else would have me because I would expect them to be like you and there just isn't anyone that good around. I just mean that a letter can't substitute for

togetherness and that's what I miss so terribly much. I'm afraid that you're going to spoil me so much until you won't have me either!"

The evening had finally arrived—*our togetherness*—and it called for a dinner date in nearby Jefferson, a quaint little town with brick streets that was a key Texas port during the mid-1800s.

I scooped up Maezie a little after six, and she nuzzled in next to me for the fifteen-minute drive up the road. She saw nothing but smiles from me because that's what filled my heart. My angel never looked more beautiful, and I told her so. We talked of missing one another and more than once I had to pull over to receive her kisses and offer my own in a contest we hoped would last a lifetime with no declared winner.

When we pulled up in front of the Stillwater Inn, I was fast out of my chair to grab the door for my lady and help her from the car.

"What is this place?" Maezie inquired, no longer sure if we were dining or...something else.

"An old turn-of-the-century home filled with antiques and supposedly the best food this side of Dallas," I replied, taking her arm in mine for the stroll up the cobblestone walkway.

"I'm impressed!" she offered. "And here I thought I knew all the eateries around these parts. I should've known you'd pull a rabbit out of your hat..."

"Oh, so you like surprises, do you?"

"Given your activities of late, let's hope so!" she teased.

"Well, then hang on a sec. I wanna show you something," I said as I reached into my front pocket.

"Not here! You could get arrested!" Maezie delivered right before the start of her mirthful laughter and the most amazing smile.

We both chuckled as I extracted the car keys and popped the trunk.

"Come closer, little girl," I teased as I opened the lid on one of several cardboard boxes arranged within. Maezie's smile faded, her eyes got big, and her mouth opened in complete surprise.

"Mackenzie Church! You did not!"

I couldn't help but smile like an idiot. I'd pulled a good one on the woman I hoped would say "yes!" in the very near future.

"Oh, yes, I did! Deal with it, woman!"

Maezie looked from me to the box of carefully wrapped antique Lenox china, white with gold backstamping, a complete collection of eight-place settings in all that had set me back more than $600 at the time (a small fortune). She took a salad plate in her hands and regarded me with a far-off, dreamy look in her eyes.

"How?"

"I took an extra job painting house numbers on curbs."

"Why?"

"Because you saw them and dreamed of them for us, and I wanted to do something extra special."

"Isn't that the cart before the horse?"

"Tell that to the damn shop owner. He'd only hold them for thirty days, and even then, I had to put down a hundred bucks. I was worried he'd sell them, and then they'd be gone forever. I wanted them for you, Maezie, cart or no cart.

She melted right then and there. Every sweaty-ass hot August day I was out painting curbs was so worth it to witness her struggle with her emotions. After carefully wrapping the salad plate back up and replacing the lid on the box, and then softly touching the tops of the other boxes in some sort of test of reality, Maezie took my face in her hands and gave me the slowest, gentlest, and most purposeful kiss I have ever received.

"I love you, Mackenzie Church," she offered in a broken warble barely above a whisper.

"And I love you, my treasure," I whispered back.

I offered Maezie my arm once more, and we made our way inside the Stillwater Inn, where the host smiled and slipped me a wink when Maezie wasn't looking.

The Stillwater was a classy place—colorful oil paintings, white tablecloths, fresh wildflowers in bud vases, heavy drapes pulled back revealing lacy sheers, padded antique chairs surrounding just the right amount of tables in the various rooms of a quaint Victorian cottage, and beeswax candles providing the perfect amount of supporting light to the dimmed chandelier that cast welcome shadows off the mantle. A low wave of my hand told the host I would seat the lady as I had in Puerto Vallarta, and in every dining experience before or since. He fluffed and placed our napkins in our laps before informing us that Greg would be tableside momentarily.

The specials were fricassee of quail with escargot in a garlic cream sauce, and herb and mustard-crusted crown rack of lamb, and the fish of the day was pompano served *en papillote*. I don't think Maezie heard a word the man was saying, she was still in LaLa Land over the china set, but the arrival of Greg with a bucket of Schramsberg Cuvée de Pinot Champagne broke her out of her reverie.

"Good evening, Mr. Church. Ma'am. My name is Greg, and I'll be taking care of you this evening. Welcome to the Stillwater Inn."

The rest of Greg's soliloquy became a soft blur as I took Maezie's hand in mine and directed all my attention upon her glowing features. I ordered the lamb and the pompano for the two of us, with marinated crab claws to start, while Greg uncorked the champagne and filled our crystal flutes.

"I'll turn in the crab claws for you and be back momentarily with fresh bread."

Greg apparently went on about his business as Maezie and I made nests in one another's eyes. So radiant. So beautiful. I couldn't wait any longer. Had we been on a playground somewhere, we both would have said "jinx!" for trying to speak at the same time. I started with her name as she started with mine, and we smiled.

"You first," I allowed.

"You amaze me, Mackenzie. Every time I try and quantify my feelings, whether in a letter to you or in person, I fail. I'm just a mess, you know? What am I going to do with you?"

"Well, I have one suggestion, but it involves a horse."

"A horse?"

Maezie actually cast a wary eye about the room, which made us both laugh and drew a smile from the couple one table over.

"Yeah, well," I stammered, my nerves trying to get the best of me. "You said the china was the cart before the horse, and you were right…"

"Oh, I was just messing with you. I just couldn't believe—"

Maezie's nervous banter gave me just enough time to extract the heirloom from my lower coat pocket and override her.

"Liesel Almay Fock," I began as Mama Julia's ring came into full view, cradled in my trembling hands and tossing light arcs off the candle in a truly mesmerizing display. "Will you accept this token as a stand in for the horse since they wouldn't let him come inside tonight? And will you please make me whole, be my bookend for life, and join my heart for always as my one true love and my wife?"

An audible gasp. Instant tears dropped from the most beautiful eyes in the world. A nod came forth before words could be found, however simple.

"Oh my god, yes." Continuous nodding. "Yes!!"

The room erupted in approval with a wave of applause as I secured the ring upon her finger. A perfect fit in every conceivable way. Somehow, I had the presence of mind to move our champagne flutes before leaning in to seal the deal, kissing first her tears before settling upon the lips that would be mine forevermore.

We eventually toasted with the champagne, and dinner was delicious as I recall. We fed each other and laughed and stared that distant stare of disbelief, and the world made sense, and we made sense, and a grand dream had just become a reality.

Much later, the stars poured through the moonroof of the Riviera on some vista overlooking Caddo Lake. The moon was fighting its way to full among the cypress trees laden heavy with Spanish moss, and we marveled at it, lost in our own world. Rachmaninoff played softly in the background, and we simply held hands, satisfied to experience our newfound oneness.

The night was perfect. Time left us alone.

25

Maezie and the Pitchfork

It felt nice to have escaped the miasma of Room 5 and to be showered and alert once more. I fully expected to awaken this morning feeling "like hammered dogshit" as my buddy Tom used to say almost every morning during those years he drank to excess but, alas, I've yet to pay the price for yesterday's fumblings. *Yet* being the operative word.

We'll see what the day holds. Better get some food in me.

I was determined to vault out of my self-imposed funk and find my way back to the land of optimism. Reliving the moments of my engagement to Maezie had put a smile on my face and lifted my mood despite the odiferous campaign my bowels were launching at the same time in the real world where the truth remained that Maezie wasn't coming to Ecuador.

"Quito!" I called out to the back of my faithful waiter as he came into view on the patio. He turned, and I tried to mimic his toothy grin just to fuck with him. I was in a surprisingly good mood given the circumstances, and that was not lost on my compadre.

"Señor Church! You are looking well this morning."

"I passed out on the beach pickled like okra but have been spared to live another day, perhaps by the gods themselves, Quito, my man. Tell me, do you have some time this afternoon to show me around? One of your tours. You pick the itinerary. I don't give a shit. I just want to get a feel for this place. I mean, that's one of the reasons I came here, and since my beloved has decided, in all her infinite wisdom, not to join me, I might as well learn a little more about your country than what Johnny Veenci told me about the fucking flag a hundred years ago."

"Yes, my afternoon is open after lunch. I am happy to take over where Mr. Veenci left off."

"That's fuckin' awesome, dude. Exactly what I want to hear. That and the sound of Café Lissadale filling up my cup. And bring me some food when you can, please. I didn't eat last night, and I'm hungry as shit."

"Sit anywhere you like, Mr. Church—"

"Call me Kenzie, Quito. Please. Mr. Church was my dad, and I'd rather not start my day off thinking about that sonofabitch right now. You figure out our itinerary and let me know what I owe you."

"Prices start at $60 for a two-hour tour of—"

"Fuck that. That's too cheap," I spewed as I took out a wad of cash and peeled off a couple of hundreds. "Here's $200 to get us started. Let me know when that runs out."

"You can pay when we are finished."

"I may be too fucked up by then, Quito. Better grab what you can now."

"As you wish, Señor Ch—Kenzie. We will start with a city tour, then we will go to Montecristi, where they make the famous hats."

I collapsed into a nice table in the shade under the watchful eyes of not one but two tyrannulet birds. Sting and Grandpa Munster were both watching from their perch as Quito upturned my coffee cup and filled it with the delicious elixir.

"Yeah, I definitely need to get me one of those Panama hats, for sure."

"The Panama hats you refer to have always been made here in Ecuador. Our country sent many as gifts for the dignitaries when the canal was first opened in Panama, and they became quite popular, and the world has come to know them by that name after your Teddy Roosevelt was photographed wearing one, but as you will see, the true craftsmen of Montecristi will amaze you with their handiwork. We will find you a nice hat, Kenzi. A very nice hat, indeed."

"See, I've learned something new already. Excellent plan, Quito. Can't wait. For now, a bowl of the melons and then a hearty breakfast, please. I need some meat. Ham, bacon, whatever you've got."

"Coming right up, Señor Church."

I gave Quito a look as he turned to scurry away, and he realized his mistake.

"Kenzie."

I nodded as an image of Judd wafted into my mind.

Oh, shit! I never finished my story! Maezie and the Pitchfork. *Here's the short version because I'm feeling pretty good at this point, and I'd like to not head back into Shittown if at all possible.*

• • •

Okay, so it was a week or so after the engagement dinner in Jefferson, and school was starting back up at Centenary. Somewhere in the interim, Maezie asked about my folks reaction to our engagement, and I told her in glorious detail about the hug I got from Madré and her kind words. Then the subject turned to Judd, and I stalled out like Jaycee right before a marathon drive to nowhere. Maezie knew in an instant that something was wrong—rarely was I at a loss for words—and over the next few minutes, she dragged it out of me.

"*Floozy?!* Your dad wouldn't know a whore if one was grinding on top of him because no woman, decent or otherwise, would go anywhere near that limp dick motherfucker!"

We were walking across campus at the time of Maezie's declaration, and I promise you, her last four words echoed throughout the quad like Lou Gehrig's famous speech at Yankee Stadium. She stopped. I stopped. We looked at each other, and I could tell both of us were imagining our religion teacher, Reverend Taylor, rounding the corner on his afternoon stroll, just in time to share in her analysis of my father's manhood, and then we laughed. Loud and hearty, because what else could we do in the moment? Maezie cussing up a storm was every bit as out of character and ridiculous as my father calling her a floozy. Still, I could tell she was hurt. And pissed. Her smile faded, and she put her hand on my arm to direct my attention to her next words.

When she finally spoke, it was in soft, measured tones. "And where might one find Mackenzie Judson Rowe Church the Turd about now, my darling?"

"Probably working on the Plymouth with Rod & Bruce."

"Would you be so kind as to motor me to him? I'd like a word with His Eminence, *The Hayride Stud*."

"Maezie...."

"No, no, dearest, I'll stop short of jeopardizing your inheritance. I merely want to afford him an opportunity to properly welcome me into your family."

"Okay, well that's a good—"

"Whether the piece of shit likes it or not! Tough titty, Trip!"

Smiles returned, we fled the quad relatively sure the delicate ears of Reverend Taylor had not been compromised, and as directed, I motored Maezie out to Pepper Ridge in short order.

I don't know that I have the words to describe the look on Judd's face when I pulled up to the garage in the Riviera, and he saw I wasn't alone. Bruce made a quick assessment of the storm a brewing and told Rod maybe they should take a break and eat their cheese sandwiches in the gazebo. Rod had never met Maezie, and he lingered for a good look, a wave, and an offering of congratulations before being hustled away by Bruce, who waved and smiled as he tugged his friend through the breezeway.

Maezie smiled back and thanked the pair.

"Top Five" I heard Scoon echo in my head as I translated Rod's eye bulging assessment of my fiancée into manspeak. Bruce just looked the way he always did when the subject of cheese sandwiches came up. And that was when it happened.

Leaning against the carport where I'd left it ten days earlier was the pitchfork I'd used to comb the cannas in search of Mama Julia's ring. Judd was frozen in place, desperately scrambling to assemble the proper words to spin his shit into something more like doo-doo. Maezie drafted her best scowl as she took up arms with the pitchfork and strode forward like Lucas McCain during the opening credits of *The Rifleman*.

"*Floozy & Burns* has a nice ring to it, don't you think?" she spoke quite clearly in his direction. "Or maybe *Flooziana Whoreride*."

Judd had no reply to this. Zero. Nada. He processed her ad-lib brilliance and offered what I knew to be an appreciative smile, one of only a few I'd ever been awarded in my life when my father had thought me particularly clever. Then again, he may have just been scared shitless, for he truly was outgunned. It seemed there was a new sheriff in town.

Maezie ditched the pitchfork a few paces before we arrived at the slack-jawed Judd and took me by the hand like she was squeezing lemons.

"The only thing I've ever wanted to steal from the Church family is your son's heart." She paused in her attack and raised our joined hands into his face, giving him a closeup view of the family heirloom now upon her finger. "But as you can see, he freely gave it to me. Perhaps, you'd like to start over."

And just like that, Judd added the clasped hands of a seasoned politician to ours, and it felt like some weird pregame football cheer was about to come forth, but instead, he said, "I misjudged you, Maezie. And for that, I'm truly sorry."

And we could tell the limp dick motherfucker really meant it.

Game. Set. Match to my wondrous fiancée.

26

Elena

"I like this van, Quito. What is it?" I inquired as we got underway on our afternoon tour.

"It is a Kia Pregio. Perfect for small tours and for my family."

"Family? You have kids?"

"Not yet, but Elena is four months along."

"Well, congratulations, brother. There's nothing greater than being a dad, I promise you. I've got a daughter just starting college, and it's been a real privilege watching her grow up. You have much to look forward to, my friend."

"Yes, this is true. It is a dream to have found my Elena, and I know she will make a wonderful mother."

'No doubt."

"I will acquaint you with a bit of the history of Manta as we drive out to Montecristi. If you have not done so, I recommend you visit the Cancebi and the Central Bank museums as both have many artifacts related to the local history.

"I haven't made it much farther than the beach and the grocery store at this point."

"Go see the museums before you leave. You will be pleased. Manta is one of the oldest cities in the region, founded by the Manteños in the mid-850s. They were a clever people who managed to avoid being conquered by the Aztecs because of a wonderful sea creature, the *spondylus*, or spiny oyster as it is known in English, even though it is not an oyster. The spondylus has a variety of very beautiful shells the Aztecs thought were from the gods, and only the Manteños knew when and where to dive for these creatures native to the area, and how to make the ceremonial masks and jewelry the wealthy found irresistible."

"Smart guys, those Manteños. Do they sell the shells now?"

"Oh, yes, there are many kinds, from just a few dollars up to several thousand for the very rare ones."

"Holy shit. I had no idea."

"Yes. They can be quite beautiful. It is easy to see why they were prized. The spondylus kept the Manteños a valuable trade partner with the Aztecs for many centuries. On the left, we are passing Tarqui Beach now, and the only way to get fish any fresher than the world famous Central

Market is to go and catch them yourself. Ecuador is tied with Spain for second place behind Thailand in the export of Pacific tuna, over a half million tons every year, shipped to Europe and the U.S. and many other places. It is a billion dollar industry for us and employs over 100,000 workers."

"Wow. You're telling me all kinds of crap I didn't know, Quito. You really know your shit."

"There is a lot to be proud of here. I am truly blessed. Ecuador is a wonderful country.

"Yes, it is, Quito. I agree."

"In a moment, we will enter into a roundabout, and I am telling you now because in the center is a statue, the Monumento a la Tejedora Manabita, that you may want a photo of. She is the hat lady, the Manabita Weaver. I won't be able to pull over, but we will pass close by as we drive to Montecristi, which is not far. The statue is just up ahead."

"Phone out. I'm ready."

"There she is."

"Oh, wow. That's a pretty serious statue!"

"Yes, she is fifteen meters tall."

"Look at her. I love her dress, and that hat looks so real!"

I managed a few quick photos of the impressive statue as we whizzed by. "Very cool. So, Quito, tell me about this lady of yours. Elena. How'd you two hook up?"

"Elena lived in my neighborhood when we were very young. There were not so many girls, mostly boys, but she was what you call a "tomboy" so she would play with us sometimes. And she was good with a hammer and was good at fixing things. We were always building forts out of old crates and whatever we could find. Elena was easy to talk to, but her father was very strict, and she had many chores, so we didn't see her much as we got older. She later told me that he would beat her when he was drunk. We would see the bruises, but we all had them from falling on rocks and just being children, so we thought nothing of it."

"Oh, that's terrible."

"And then one day, she was gone. The whole family. Her father had trouble keeping a job, and he lost their home, and we didn't know where they went. She wasn't in school anymore, and my parents told me they moved to another city and not to worry, that everything would be all right. But I did worry. It cost me many sleepless nights as a boy. I look back now and see I was very much in love with her."

"How old were you at the time?"

"Nine or ten. After Elena left, I kept mostly to myself and did more chores for the family, so I'd have more time to think of her while I worked. I became quite the loner, but also more responsible, and my work for the family allowed my parents to grow their produce business and we prospered. So, in many ways, it was a good thing. Not Elena's leaving, of course—"

"No, I get it. You found your work ethic and that helped your family."

"Yes. Exactly. Eventually, time softened my memories of Elena, and I began to date in my later school years. Some. But none of the girls were like her. Elena captured something of my heart the others could not reach."

"Oh, I hear ya. That's the way it was for me with Maezie, the girl that was supposed to meet me here."

"I am sorry for you. I was lucky to find Elena again. I cannot imagine if she had not wanted to be with me."

"Oh, Maezie wants to be with me, Quito, but she's married to another man—husband number three—and her loyalty to her commitment won't let her leave, no matter how much I tempt her. She spoke of retiring here in Ecuador one day because it seemed so beautiful and our dollar would go much further, and so I hopped on a plane and came down to check it out, maybe buy a place. And I told her, and she said we just needed to make it happen, but that was the alcohol talking, I guess. This guy she's married to—he's not horrible but.... We're fuckin' meant to be together! Hell, I tried to put Maezie behind me, tried for a life with someone else. I got married, tried to mold her into someone like Maezie, but there was an age difference, and she grew into her own woman. It just didn't work. I got an amazing daughter out of the deal, though, so I really can't complain. And now, it's just hard to see paradise right in front of you and not be able to reach it. Y'know?"

"Yes, señor, I do. Too many years, I was searching for Elena in the eyes of other women. Fate took pity on me, and I was conducting a tour of the hat factory we are going to now when I hear someone call out *'Elena!'* and my heart stops as it always does when I hear that name, and this young woman has a briefcase in her hand, and she is running after another woman, and I know right away the one she is calling to is my Elena."

"No way! Whad'ja do?!"

"I stop the tour and I, too, call out for Elena, and she does not know where to look first, but then our eyes meet, and she knows it is me just as I know it is her. And she cries out *'Bollito!'* because that is her special name for me, and we come together, and I was glad the tour was almost over because I was a very poor guide after that."

"What a great story! So, you two got together and you made her Mrs. Quishpe!"

"Well, yes. Eventually. Elena was married at the time to a man who...had a great love for himself...."

"A narcissist."

"Yes, that is the word. Thank you. Elena had worked very hard in life and had achieved her dream to be an architect, but she did not have much love for herself and gave her efforts to this man who did not care who it was filling his ego, and he kept her from her friends, and began to treat her quite poorly. She looked very tired to me, and I could feel her tears were of joy, but they held much sadness as they kept coming. Too much sadness. The pain in my heart I had always had for her was back again, but this time the woman stood before me. So, I know this pain you speak of now with your lady. I just wanted her pain to stop, and

I wanted us to have the beautiful life I knew we could have."

"Oh, man, Quito. You're singing my song, for sure. So, what happened?"

"As Elena tells it, just having me in her life became this light of joy. Just being able to call me from work or mail me a card helped her feel connected to something again. And I was overjoyed, Kenzie. I would use every opportunity to remind Elena what an amazing person she is. But I struggled with being in the way, too, because the ego man saw that she was being happy, and he thought she had found a lover at work, and he became more angry and yelled all the time.

"Eventually, I found out and did not like knowing there was such a price she was having to pay for the happiness I was bringing to her. I did not know what to do. We both were miserable. Until, one day, he came to her work and tore through her desk and found cards from me and went into a rage. He picked up a building model, her favorite project, and he threw it at her, and it smashed apart. The security came and threw him out, and that was it for Elena. She thought of her father and the beatings and said, 'No more!' She had her big cousins get her things and she left the ego man. And she divorced him. I did not know this at the time. I would call her work, and they said she was on holiday, and I waited. Then one day, I am serving lunch at the hotel, and she is suddenly there. And this time her tears were relief and joy. And I held her, and I will never let her heart go again. Never."

"Aww, dude, that's fuckin' awesome. I didn't mean to bring up bad memories, but that's a really beautiful story. I wish you two every possible happiness as you start your family together."

"I thank you and wish you the same fate with your Maezie. I think it will come to pass. God is very good if we can learn to get out of his way."

"I'll drink to that. Speaking of, how much longer to Montecristi? I could use a beer."

"Five minutes. It is just ahead. I know the owner of Beer Point. He is a cousin of mine. We will stop there first."

"Beer Point. I'm liking the sound of that, for sure."

27

Hellos and Goodbyes

The first reunion moment happened at a mini mart in Kilgore, Texas, in the almost summer of '95. It was magical.

"We can't meet at my work," Maezie had wisely reasoned. "School's still in session for another week. But there's a mini mart on Airport Road. You'll see it. It's out there all by itself. I'll gas up there, and we can take your car somewhere. I know an amazing pastry shop or...who knows. We'll figure it out."

While I'm a nut for well-made pastries of any kind, food was the last thing on my mind as Maezie and I plotted our first in-person meeting since the spring of 1982. Here we were, now at the end of May, thirteen years later, and I'd managed to find her. And we were hell-bent on seeing one another.

Five years earlier, when I was still living on the west coast, I'd received a copy of the alumni directory from Centenary in the mail and had immediately looked up Maezie. In the decade before Google hit the world stage, the book afforded a rare opportunity to locate people from my college days, and Maezie certainly topped that list. My roommate, Weaz (short for Weasel, which he was on so many levels), and I had consumed a twelve-pack and counting that Saturday afternoon, and he encouraged me to call the phone number listed for her, even though she was boasting a different last name that, once again, wasn't mine. *Potter*. Another beer or several later, I called as Weaz stood by to cheer me on but mostly eavesdrop on what would be my first contact with Maezie since college. On the third ring, the hubby answered, and I had a mini panic attack, which was quickly overridden by my burning desire to talk to her no matter how briefly. When I asked if she was there, the hubby confirmed that she was, and then he asked who was calling.

"Jaycee," I replied. "I'm an old friend from college."

Just covering my ass, people.

"Hello?" Maezie came on the line sounding a bit confused.

"Maezie, it's Kenzie."

Tailgating the mention of my name was her squealing reply, an 11 on the 1-to-10 volume setting for a landline.

"I knew it! I thought, what in the hell would Jaycee ever be calling me for, then I thought maybe he was driving my way. Oh, no! Then I could hear it in my mind, you imitating that frightening laugh of his, and I thought, it had to be you. Oh, my god, Kenzie, how are you?"

Hours later, Weaz and I picked apart the phone conversation and the remains of our case of Lucky Lager. Maezie shared that she'd divorced Hubby Number One four years earlier. It was a horrendous extrication that involved numerous restraining orders and resulted in Maezie going underground for several years. Hearing the details broke my heart, especially since I'd driven her right into his arms.

• • •

It was maybe an ordinary Wednesday night in February of '82, and I was walking Maezie back to her dorm room after suffering a less-than-marginal meal at the Caf.

"That might've been the worst spaghetti I've ever had. Gooshy, starchy, overcooked crap," Maezie complained.

"Lousy impasta!" I said in the worst possible Mafia-guy accent.

"I'm telling you," Maezie laughed, "you could be the next Carson."

"Not with that schtick, I'm afraid," I assured her. "Thank you. But a) he'll never retire, and b) I've got a clothing empire to run."

And that's when I stepped in it.

While Judd had finally come around to the idea of me taking Maezie as my bride, there was still the matter of the throne I was expected to assume, and it was a sticking point with my beloved. Maezie jammed on the brakes, turned and faced me with a storm brewing in her eyes.

"Since when? What happened to Colorado?"

I should have scrambled for the high ground since this earth had been turned more than once, but nooooooooo.

"Seriously? I can't just pick up and leave, Maezie. The store's been in the family for almost a hundred years. It would absolutely kill my mom. I mean, maybe someday, but it looks like we'll be starting out in Shreveport next May. Which is probably better because our folks aren't getting any younger, and your gran is what? Seventy-seven now? It's not forever...."

"Well, since you put it that way," Maezie began with more than a note of sarcasm that I just completely missed.

"Thank you," I said, relieved and thinking I'd squirmed out of that one unscathed.

"I mean, it's far better to kill off *our* dreams than risk upsetting our elders, who've had decades to live their best lives," she concluded.

"Maezie, c'mon. You know my hands are tied."

"We're talking marriage, Kenzie. Serious stuff. Mark: 10, Verse 7, 'For this cause shall a man leave his father and mother and cleave to his wife.'"

"What about: *Honor thy father and thy mother?* That's a commandment!"

"It doesn't say to sacrifice your life. Grow some balls, Kenzie! First, the fraternity, and now this. When are you ever going to stand up for yourself? For us!"

"What do you think that ring is all about? Do you have *any* idea what it took for me to put it there?"

"Such a burden."

"Commitment!"

Something broke in Maezie in that moment, and she took a stand. Strangely enough, so did I.

"Forgive me if I don't see it, Kenzie," she said with angry defiance as she worked Mama Julia's ring from her finger and held it aloft to underscore her point. "Here. Add this to your stupid, fucking empire."

"What the *hell* are you doing? I shouted. "No, Maezie...no."

I snatched the ring from her hand and shoved it back in place, back on the only home I wanted that heirloom to ever have.

"Don't you ever do that shit again."

"Or what?" she fired back.

I don't know if I even tried to answer. I was back in my childhood, the first time I'd ever seen *The Wizard of Oz*, and the Wicked Witch has just unleashed the winged monkeys, and they've landed on the Scarecrow and are tearing the shit out of his stuffing.

By now, Maezie and I were standing in front of her dorm, and the silence of my nightmare was shattered by a loud bang as the push bar of the front door was punched open, and a tiny woman escaped past us into the night. The slamming of that door followed as the woman's hulking boyfriend lumbered past us in hot pursuit.

"Get back here, Cindy!" he shouted. The hulk I knew as Tony caught the girl and yanked her around to face him. "This is *crazy*, and you know it."

"You're hurting me, Tony!"

"Hurting *you*? You're crushing my balls in a vice over some petty garbage."

For her part, Cindy managed to break free, but Tony was right on her ass and caught her again, slamming her up against the building.

"Listen to me. I love you, Cindy. You! No one else. There is no one else."

"You don't look at me the same," Cindy whimpered.

"I've had a lot on my mind. I... I'm failing Calculus, babe. I.... I was ashamed to tell you. If I lose my scholarship—"

Cindy put her hand to Tony's mouth to silence him. "Oh, Tony. I'm so sorry. I had no idea. I feel like such a fool..."

"No, honey. No. I'm the fool. I can't lose you, Cindy. I just can't."

This kind of shit happened more than once with the volatile couple, but in that moment, they found peace.

Cindy studied Tony and eventually smiled. "Oh, Tony. You do care. You really do."

It was a melodramatic moment right out of *West Side Story*, but I'd been glad for the distraction, however temporary. The happy couple kissed and returned to the dorm arm in arm once more.

"There!" Maezie pointed. "That's what I'm talking about, Kenzie."

"Are you kidding me? Tony Krantz is a hothead, a loose cannon. Did you see the way he yanked her around?"

"He was fighting for her. For them!"

"He shoved her into the building, Maezie. He hurt her."

"Why do you have to be so passive all the time? Fight for us!"

I was in no mood for introspection or, rather, I couldn't see myself for shit. "Jesus was passive. Gandhi. Dr. King. What's wrong with that?"

That drew a big sigh from Maezie, which I took as a partial victory, but she was just floored that I would compare myself to the Mt. Rushmore of peaceful prophets.

"Nothing, Kenzie. They stood by their principles and didn't back down. That's my point. What are you standing for?"

I was pinned in, defeated, and decided to do something totally out of character. It was anger, it was frustration, it was bewilderment, it was I don't know what the fuck. I grabbed Maezie by the shoulders and shoved her back two feet into a pine tree.

"Happy now?" I said as she reached for the back of her head, a look of total shock on her face. In an instant, whatever part of me that thought I could be Tony collapsed, and I started crying out of genuine remorse as Maezie looked down at her bloody fingertips.

"Oh, god, Maezie, I'm so sorry. Are you all right?"

She didn't say a damn thing.

"I can't do this. I'm not Tony. I'll never be Tony...."

Maezie regarded me softly. "I'm not asking you to be. I just need you to stand up for us."

"One hundred years. It's not that simple."

"It should be."

"My mother lost her parents and her daughter in one night, Maezie. I cannot even imagine the pain of that loss, and I was the *lucky one* that survived the fire. Try that on for size. And now, I'm going to kill off her family legacy, just like that, huh? Sure. Why not? Simple decision...."

"It's for the future, Kenzie, not the past. You can't help what happened that night. You were ten, for god's sake. It's time to move on."

"I...I need time to think."

"Take all the time you need. In the meantime, I guess you'll be wanting this back."

Maezie tugged the engagement ring from her finger and offered it up once more. This time, though, I took it.

"You know what...I guess I do," I said as the color drained from my face. I could see the monkeys flying away with my stuffing, leaving me for dead. I turned from the one woman I had ever truly loved in my twenty-one years on Planet Earth, and I walked away in silence, stumbling along as the constant stream of tears made any sort of purposeful stride impossible.

• • •

Maezie and I spent over two and a half hours on the phone that day in California. The hubby was not amused by our little auld lang syne celebration, and it was beyond time for us to say goodbye, preferably forever, as far as he was concerned. After an awkward silence, we made some vague promise to get together if I ever found my way back from the west coast, which led to a final question.

"So, I have to ask," Maezie said in an attempt to address the elephant in the room. "What happened to Fleming & Burns? Dad told me it closed a while back."

"Yeah, Judd sold it to this hot shot insurance guy who screwed it up within the first year. Defaulted on the payments, bank foreclosed. We lost the building, the money, everything."

"Oh, my god! How is that even possible?"

"Sometime when you've got a spare day or two, I'll tell you. Suffice it to say that when it all went down, Judd had to sell his precious *Hayride* to fund their retirement. It was not a pretty thing."

"Oh, I'm so sorry to hear that. So, why did he sell the store in the first place? What happened to you running the empire?"

And that's when we arrived at the ironic moment of this whole tale. I hesitated, perhaps a bit too long, as my mind worked to anticipate how Maezie would digest the forthcoming revelation.

"Hello?" she spoke into the silence.

"So...after we broke up," I began, "I was talking with my mom, and she asked me about my plans for the future, and I just unloaded on her."

"You *yelled* at the Supreme Madré?"

I smiled. It was so comforting to share that familiarity with Maezie. We were back in time so effortlessly.

"No, no. I just laid it all out there, about my frustrations with Barbunzo, and Judd losing interest, and somehow, I came clean about my feelings. I basically told her I was bored with the store, and it didn't really suit me."

"Oh, no. Was she devastated?"

"No, that's just it. She told me that no one had a gun to my head, that I was free to pursue whatever interested me, and that her father only ran the store because he could get a paycheck and stay out on the lake all day fishing. I couldn't believe that shit."

There was a silence that followed. Gears turned. Reality closed in. I don't know if I was letting Maezie have time to process, or if I was just out of words. Or maybe ashamed. No, in that moment, I realized we'd both been fighting for the same thing—commitment. And we'd both failed. For me, the test had been the ring and what it symbolized. For her, it was my inability to put us first in all of life's decisions—no matter what. That was our breakup in a nutshell. There was nowhere to hide, no words of apology that could put a dent in my remorse. I eventually found the need to add a postscript, choosing to imitate my mother's unmistakable drawl to help soften the blow.

"*I was happy living in Virginia, happy to have escaped this god-awful humidity,*" I said in Madre's twang and vernacular. "*It was your father's idea to come back here not mine. Run the store or do like he did and find somebody else to. Or you two can sell it. I don't care one way or the other.*"

Maezie laughed softly as my mother came to life on the phone call. Or maybe it was just a *hunh*, a marker of that shitty moment in time that stood out like a cheap tombstone among the mausoleums of the rich and famous. Not the best way to end our reunion phone call, but then again, maybe it was merciful.

"So, what I want to know, K-man, is why Maezie didn't seek you out after Marriage #1 tanked," Weaz asked me almost as soon as I hung up the phone. "What'd she say about that?"

"Bro, she was shocked that I even called her today. She thought I hated her with a passion."

"What?"

"That's what she said. Get this. You're not gonna believe this shit. After we broke up, there was this girl, Avalon–"

"Oh, I like this story already."

"Hang on. It gets pretty shitty. This girl Avalon goes to Centenary, and she's pretty hot in her own weird way. Kinda punk rock, kinda Goth. Dresses mismatch crazy, doesn't give a shit about what anyone thinks—an artsy Madonna type. I come in to work one day at Fleming & Burns, and there she is. Turns out she'd been hired for temp work by the store. Every year in February we'd do inventory, a real pain in the ass, and she heard about it through a friend and signed up, so there she was.

"Well, shit, I'm feelin' sorry for myself, and she's quirky and funny, and so I pair off with her, and we're countin' socks and stupid shit like that, and we get to know each other. Lunchtime comes, and I take her with me, and the fun continues. I get Avalon all to myself for a week, and I'm startin' to dig this chick. She's no Maezie, but we can have a little fun, and I don't have to map out our future or anything like that, so we have a pretty good time."

"So Maezie saw you two together and that was that?"

"No, far worse. Avalon was in this play at school, had the female lead. And so, me being me, I send over some flowers, and she gets 'em, and all is good for another week until her boyfriend returned from some volleyball tour and that was the end of that."

"Boyfriend?"

"Yeah. Apparently, I was just a place saver. I wasn't too broken up about it because my head and heart were still with Maezie, but it fucked with me, y'know?"

"Oh, I hear ya."

"So, I just laid low the rest of the semester, poured myself into the fraternity, and they were glad to have their entertainer back, and I was glad for the distraction all the guys afforded me. Felt like family. I grew up an only child for the most part and, I don't know. It felt like family is all I can say. Next thing I know, somebody tells me Maezie's dating this dweeby orchestra dude, a violinist like her. A fuckin' freshman! And I'm thinking, *This shit ain't gonna last.* But it does, at least until the end of the semester. And then it hits me: Maezie didn't jack around in college like I did, so she's done. She graduates and she's off. Next thing I know, I find out she's married the dude. All the fights about my fuckin' job, and she marries some freshman dweeb who sacks groceries for a living. Literally.

"I could see where Maezie would think I hated her. I was definitely pissed and confused as hell. She even said on the phone that she figured I felt sorry for her, and I definitely did, but I never stopped loving her."

"So, finish the story...."

"Oh, yeah. So, she tells me just now that she had an elective left in her final semester. Some sewing class she was taking for an easy A. I remembered that, but then she tells me the class project involved working in the theater department helping with the costuming."

"Uh-oh..."

"Yeah, uh-oh. Maezie was working in the back the day the flowers came in for Avalon, and I was being all cutesy, addressing the card, *To a star of tomorrow!* Well, Avalon hadn't showed up yet, so the delivery guy left them. And Maezie's suitemate, Annette, comes along and sees the card and recognizes my printing from all the cards and flowers

I'd left for Maezie in the past, so she snatches them up and goes running to Maezie."

"Oh, fuck, dude."

"I had no idea until she told me a few minutes ago, bro. Maezie was all excited, tore open the card...and saw it wasn't for her. And it just crushed her. She started dating the freshman right after that. Told me she did it to spite me. Can you believe that? Then she ends up marrying the guy and gets pregnant, thinking the whole family thing will settle her mind and give her the *happily ever after* she was looking for from me, but it all goes to shit instead."

"Oh, man...."

"She stuck with him because she said that's what she learned from our breakup. And they limped along a couple of years until he became abusive...and Maezie left and divorced his ass."

"Holy shit, bro."

"Eventually, some friends from her work hooked her up with this Potter guy because he's just some regular guy with a good heart who was respected in the community, and that's all Maezie wanted at that point—someone who was stable and would treat her decently. Fuck the knight-in-shining-armor thing. They started dating, and she got pregnant, and so they married."

"Fuck, man, if you'd just known."

"I know, bro. She said, '*He's a nice man, pretty boring, not funny like you, but he's a good provider.*' And I could tell she wasn't even selling that shit to herself as she spoke it. She sounded like the way I felt as a kid when my parents told me to go give Great Aunt Bertha a hug and a kiss. Nice old lady, but I didn't give a shit about her. Maezie sounds resigned. Most of me is just selfishly pining away for her, but that part makes me sound really pathetic. She's had a couple of boys with the guy, plus her daughter from Number One, and she just puts all her love into her kids, it sounds like. Maybe that'll be enough."

"You really believe that?"

"Honestly? No. But I've never had kids either."

"That's some heavy shit, K-man," Weaz offered in summation.

And that was all the contact I had with Maezie for the next five years.

28
Bollito

"Kilgore's not a very big town," Maezie had told me in her preamble to suggesting the mini mart for our point of rendezvous. "Mr. Potter's pretty well known, and people talk so, innocent or no, we've got to be careful."

There was nothing innocent about what transpired when we finally saw each other in the almost summer of 1995. We both were competing with our memories of love and anxious to give breathing room to our lust-laden phone conversation.

Maezie was every runway model, every hair tossing Herbal Essence commercial girl, every Bolero singing, braided-hair perfect 10 when she stepped from her deep-blue Chevy Suburban that afternoon in an amazing flowery peach ensemble, a walking Monet. It was all I could do to maintain any composure at all as I watched her face light up like the Christmas tree at Rockefeller Center. I don't think she spoke, and I sure as hell didn't because we would've had to relax our ridiculous smiles to do so.

I'd already choreographed our first hug in my mind when I finally emerged from my Jeep Cherokee, same deep-blue color, and went to meet her. But that plan flew out the window when we both buried our faces in one another. It was like our skin was on fire and the meeting of our lips was the only hope of extinguishing the blaze. It was minutes. It was hours. It was the pearly gates of Heaven swinging open wide.

Kilgore was going to have a shit ton to talk about now. And neither of us cared.

• • •

"Okay! We are all gassed up," Quito offered behind one of his trademark grins as he piled back into the Kia. "Next stop, Beer Point!"

I don't know what kind of expression I was wearing since I'd been to Hell and back with my memories during the five minutes it had taken him to gas us up at the Terpel station.

"Are you all right, Kenzie?" he inquired. "You smile but there are tears."

"Yeah, Quito, I'm fine. Just, y'know, thinking about the past. Good mixed with the bad."

"Well, it looks like the good ones are winning."

"Yeah. Hey, lemme ask you something. What do your friends call you? Quito is your tour name but...."

"Most call me Javi, short for Javier."

"Can I call you Javi?"

"Yes, of course."

"And what does Elena call you?"

"Bollito. It means *'cookie'* in Spanish."

"Ohhhhh, cookie. Like a little treat, huh?"

"Elena called me that in childhood, making fun of my other name, Fortunato. She said I was like a fortune cookie to her because I would give her things to dream about when we talked."

"Oh, man, that's sweet. *Bollito.* I like it. So, changing the subject, what's the popular beer here, Javi?"

"Pilsener and Club are the biggest, but many local beers are becoming quite popular."

"Yeah, that's what I meant to say. I want something local. I don't like hoppy beers, just something smooth and nice."

"Perhaps a San Blas, then. They make a very smooth porter. We will let my cousin Bennie decide. He will know."

"Well, let's go see what Bennie has to say, Javi, my man."

29

The Not-from-Panama Hat

"Two fucking thousand dollars! My cowboy hat cost me five hundred, and I thought that was insane, but that was for some machine-made bullshit. So, yeah, two grand, okay."

"You look like a very important man, Kenzie."

"I'm tellin' ya, after seeing the process that goes into making one of these fuckin' things," I rambled on as I touched the brim of my Fedora style not-from-Panama hat, "I mean, shit, yeah, it's worth two grand, easy. A fuckin' year to make one. All by hand! All that washing and picking out the fibers and the weaving and ironing and shaping. Hell, yeah. I just gotta get the damn thing home in one piece now. But you gotta admit, Javi, this is one badass hat. Way better than that cheap shit they're hawking on the beaches. And to find one that'll fits my big-ass head is amazing in and of itself. Good call, bro. And a helluva tour, too. Fascinating!"

"You needed that hat, señor. It looks very nice on you and will afford you important shade from the sun from now on."

"Am I going to regret not springing the full four grand for the ultra-smooth, top-of-the-line, super badass one, though, Javi? I mean, shit. What's another two grand at this point? Maezie's not coming. I'm saving money there...."

And just like that, I went quiet. Four San Blas porters with Bennie on an empty stomach might not have been the best idea I'd ever had. But, damn, it sure made the tour of the Montecuador Hat Company a really good time.

"I agree that it was, perhaps, too dressy for your needs. I think you made the perfect choice," my new friend Javi, the former Quito, assured me.

"Fuck it. It's done. No regrets, Javi. No regrets about anything," I said as I pulled the brim a little lower over my eyes and contemplated a siesta. "Hey, can we stop somewhere and get some food? I need to eat something before we go to—where the hell are you taking me next?"

"The Seva chocolate factory."

"Right! I definitely need food before we get there, or I'll gorge myself like some Oompa-Loompa, and nobody wants to see that shit. Trust me."

"Yes, of course. Would you like to sample local food?"

"Yeah, absolutely. Nothing too weird, but I'm open to whatever."

"I will take you to Mami Nina's. You will like it."

"Sounds perfect," I said as my thoughts turned once more to Maezie. *God, please let her change her mind....*

• • •

There was a sensation of tunnel vision as everything surrounding Maezie and me at the mini mart was reduced to a blur. We kissed for minutes, hands on faces, necks, shoulder blades, waists. And then the tennis match began, eyes consumed with passion searched for and found their mates in one another. Maezie's eyes bored right into my soul, and I welcomed the invasion.

We studied, verified, verified again. It was, oh, so real. I opened my mouth to tell her I loved her, always had, always would, but she shushed me with a finger, perhaps knowing that the verbal admission would be too much in that moment. More studying. My god, I was lost, so very lost in her. My chest was about to explode from sheer joy.

And then, she spoke.

"We gotta go. Take me away from here," she said as she took my hand and led me toward the Jeep.

I prayed she meant forever, but I knew better. *She's a married woman. A mom!* Her hand in mine...so silky. The fit was perfect. I held to her like the world's strongest magnet, refusing to let go, even when I'd delivered her to my passenger door, and then only after making her pay the toll of more kissing did I release her to slip into the seat.

"C'mon," she finally said, taking the door handle. I stared at Maezie's overwhelming beauty for an endless expanse of time. And she let me.

"God, how I've missed you," she said a minute or so after her eyes had said their fill.

We somehow ended up over at the damn pastry shop, but by then the reality of our earlier display had put Maezie on high alert. She ran in and got us two apple strudels to go and told me to drive toward Longview, just somewhere out into the country. The only thing I didn't like about the strudel, besides the fact that flakes were now littering my shirt like giant dandruff, was that it didn't leave me with a free hand, so I inhaled it before we got more than a few blocks on our trip to nowhere, then reached once more for the hand that belonged in mine.

"You look absolutely stunning," I told her between stolen glances at the road, just enough to keep us on the pavement and safe from other traffic. The highlights in her hair lit up her face, or maybe that was just the glow we'd created.

Maezie thanked me, then asked the question only she could, in the way only she could ask it. "What the hell are we doing?"

It was accompanied by the biggest, most joyful smile that, for me, immediately filed her query in the rhetorical category. She grabbed my bicep with both hands and leaned into me, resting her head on my shoulder. Yeah, definitely rhetorical.

"The time has come," the Walrus said,

"To talk of many things
Of shoes — and ships — and sealing-wax —
Of cabbages — and kings —
And why the sea is boiling hot — and whether pigs have wings," I offered, pleased with my recall of an almost forgotten poem.

"Lewis Carroll," Maezie quietly mused. "Am I the Walrus or the Carpenter?"

"Oh, shit," I offered. "I stepped in that one, didn't I?"

Maezie and I enjoyed driving and talking for the next hour or so, getting caught up on life. Laughing and crying, going over every painful detail of our breakup and where we should have zigged rather than zagged. If nothing else, we both understood "*why the sea is boiling hot.*"

Neither of us had any answers about the future at the conclusion of our outing, but I'd discovered she was bound and determined to honor the vows she'd made in marriage, for I had shown her in my own determined actions that night in front of her dorm a strength that far outshined any muscle play by Tony Krantz. And she had listened. Maezie always listened.

There were times I thought to stop, to pull the car over and give in to the desires of my heart, and there were plenty of times Maezie's eyes encouraged me, but when I was weak, she was strong. And when she was weak, I became a better man. I began to hate myself for the total devotion I held for that woman, for my willingness to stand in the archway of her marriage and family and tempt her heart as only I could, knowing that if I got my way, we would forever alter the lives of her children and open the door of infidelity, inviting it to lurk in the corner of our shared existence for the rest of our days.

Maezie thought as I did, exactly as I did, and that theme would overshadow any and all reunions to follow.

30

The Summer of '95

Life, it seemed, had no hope of returning to normal as we approached the summer of '95.

Maezie had a week or so left of teaching at the local high school—orchestra, naturally, and I saw that purely for the opportunity that it was: to see her, absorb her, feel her permeate my otherwise meaningless existence. I made the hour and half drive every morning for a five-minute rendezvous in the outer parking lot before she started her day. I certainly had nothing better to do, nothing in my schedule that couldn't be delayed for three hours and five minutes for the chance to start my day with a singing heart and a glorious smile. Given our surroundings, we could only talk, with me playing the role of some concerned parent appearing to quiz her about finals or some such shit. Our eyes, however, betrayed hearts that were back at the mini mart while our brains were clearly in absentia.

The Fourth of July fell on a Tuesday that summer, so the festivities were observed by most folks in the nation on the previous Saturday, the first. I ended up in Sulphur Springs, Texas, of all places, because the fireworks going on between Maezie and me simply could not be contained.

She and two of her top students were sitting in with the East Texas Symphony Orchestra for the annual Independence Day concert in Heritage Square, and the four-and-a-half-hour drive was nothing to me. I knew she would be *sans family*, so I seized upon the event she'd mentioned casually the last day of the school year as an ideal place to steal another sliver of precious time.

The presence of her students kept the visit within proper bounds, as Maezie worked hard to spin a believable story as to who I was and how I ended up in Sulphur Springs. I don't recall her words from that day, but the later admonishment I remember, so it must've been quite the tap dance for her. I took some pictures of the boys and had them take a few of us, and I snuck a few shots of the orchestra in action, so I came away from the event feeling like a pirate lording over a great treasure. I had current photos of Maezie and me together. Solid gold.

A few weeks later, I was shocked to see Maezie's blue Suburban turn into the driveway at Pepper Ridge one afternoon as I was returning from the mailbox. Her daughter, who was now twelve, sat in the passenger seat. Maezie met me down the driveway, and we hugged. She whispered that the two of them were on an afternoon shopping spree and the car just somehow drove itself east to Shreveport. I was thrilled to see her and to meet her daughter, however briefly. It felt good to know I wasn't the only helpless addict.

The pre-teen knew me only as some friend of her mama's, I think, but children pay a hell of a lot more attention than we give them credit for, and when her mama finally put the Suburban in reverse and headed back to Kilgore, I was later informed the daughter commented on our parting hug, stating matter-of-factly, "He didn't want to let you go. That man really loves you."

Fast forward nine years, dear reader, and this would be the site of my one and only wedding. Did I think of Maezie in 2004 as I stood not more than forty feet away and promised myself to Not Maezie? At some point, yes.

But during that precious afternoon back in the summer of 1995, which still competes in my memory of defining moments from the front yard at Pepper Ridge, something about meeting one of Maezie's kids began to work on me, and I was sure it worked on her as well.

It would all come to a head the following weekend in San Antonio.

• • •

"Hey, Kenzie! You awake over there?" Javi asked, jolting me from my daydream.

"Yeah, man. I'm here."

"I could not tell with that fancy new brim pulled over your eyes."

"Yeah, I'm livin' the life now, Javi, that's for sure."

"I hope you are hungry. Mami Nina's is just up ahead."

"Thank god, I'm starving."

Granted, our late lunch / early dinner spot was a much better choice than having me gorge myself on chocolate, but I still left Mami Nina's feeling (and probably looking) like an Oompa-Loompa. I had this amazing Corvina fish breaded in I-don't-know-what, with lentils and rice, fried plantains, shrimp ceviche, and more food than I could possibly eat. Javi had the world's largest burrito, and the sonofabitch ate the whole damn thing. Well, less a fairly good-sized bite from me, but still. I was impressed!

We waddled out of there and migrated to the car to head toward to chocolate factory. I should have saved room.

Fuck it! I'd make room!

Both of us were stuffed, though, so the car fell silent for the ten-minute drive to chocolate paradise, and I drifted back to the summer of '95.

• • •

Maezie had given me an earful about her upcoming boring-ass teacher conference when we were chatting in my driveway, dropping hints like hankies at a debutante ball. That year's conference was scheduled for San Antonio, one of the places she and I had escaped to back in the day as a warmup to the Puerto Vallarta trip, so we had a history with the famous Texas city and its Riverwalk. *Remember the Alamo!* they are fond of saying down there, and I did, but for vastly different reasons.

The girl had a phone in her car, which was pretty cutting edge for 1995. I didn't have shit, so I called her car phone from a payphone when I arrived in the city. She was not surprised I was there, nor was I, but we both squealed with delight as we contemplated the next twenty-four hours together.

We met at the Riverwalk and enjoyed an afternoon of strolling hand in hand, laughing and shopping and people watching. Lord, how we loved to people watch! I'd start with some grumbling an old man might be making, and she'd jump in with the fussing of his missus, and we'd make up lives and backstories and laugh until we could hardly breathe. I felt alive.

It was pretty hot in San Antonio, but there was a nice breeze along the river. Maezie lingered over a pair of earrings in a gift shop, and I took note. She turned down an aisle and grabbed my arm and pulled me in front of the most realistic plaster sculpture of a rooster I'd ever seen.

"Look, isn't this amazing!"

I had to agree. The rooster was a dark, almost eggplant color, with hints of green, a corn-yellow yoke, and a very red crown. The eyes were so realistic that I felt like I was being watched.

"I wonder how much they want for it. I'd love to put that in my kitchen. The kids would think it's hysterical."

I reached over and flipped the tag on one of Rooster Boy's yellow talons.

"Five hundred eighty-five smackeroonies," I declared.

Maezie cast a wary eye about before taking me into her confidence. "Fuck a whole lotta that, then."

The gal still had perfect timing. We busted out laughing as we made our exit and continued on our merry way.

We steered clear of the Polo Dirt Chicken at Casa Rio that evening, instead splitting an order of supreme nachos and a botanas platter of stuffed jalapeños, mini-quesadillas, and chicken poppers. Two frozen margaritas each, and we were both nicely lit. Make that somewhat trashed.

I think we got a little loud a time or two because the waiter asked us if we were ready for the check not once but thrice. But we had people watching to do. There were many patrons that had yet to serve as our entertainment, and we held court for close to two hours.

"Fuck 'em," Maezie said at one point when the bill finally arrived, with another round of margaritas on it. It was time for us to make our exit. Translation: stagger back to the hotel.

We eventually arrived at the Crockett Hotel after some more leisurely window shopping, and Maezie handed me the key to the room and told me, "It's over there somewhere."

Room 505 was spacious and clean. We tucked ourselves away and kicked off our shoes as the train of reality began to pull into the station. Slowly. Very slowly.

We began to kiss and, oh my god, what ensued may have been enhanced by our slightly inebriated state, but I wouldn't bet my life on it. We were back at Cara Mia's that first night, only the legendary first kiss was now in super slow motion. There was something fluid about the way our mouths fit together, and our tongues probed. No time had passed, no starting anew. This was beyond the mini mart. This was passion on some angelic, professional level, delivered with exquisite precision, igniting every possible nerve ending and causing our bodies to move in ways theretofore thought impossible.

I pressed Maezie's tailbone into me, trying to merge the rest of us into the single unit our mouths had succeeded in doing. She lifted a leg and tucked it behind mine as she clawed my glutes and pushed me deeper into her eager hips. A great sexual ballet began to unfold as our bodies disappeared into familiar surroundings. So soft were her lips, so moist her gums, so demanding of my tongue was this entity consuming me in totality. Bliss.

"No!" the shout came without warning, followed by the shove.

I flew backward and bounced off the bed like one of those inflatable Bozo Bop Bags I had when I was a kid.

Maezie had a look about her that was still hard for me to describe. There were elements of a punch-drunk boxer, a thoughtful philosopher, and the sexiest woman to ever walk the planet.

When my Bozo bounce landed me on the floor, her bewilderment dissolved into more laughter, and I had to admit the whole *passion-to-punchin'* transition was pretty damn funny. She reached out a hand to pull me up, and I wasn't the least bit sorry when I pulled her down onto the carpet with me.

"What the hell was that?"

"You know exactly what the hell that was, Kenzie. We can't be doing that shit. I'm a married woman, with kids. Forbidden fruit."

"It was just a little nibble," I offered meekly with the best sly smile I could manage in the moment.

"Tell that to him," she said as she pointed out the obvious rise in my Levi's.

"I would, but he never listens."

"Don't I know it," Maezie thought aloud. "Did, anyway," she continued quietly as she used the bed to pull herself up and then reached back and helped me regain my footing. She studied me for a moment and relaxed into her signature cuteness, her tongue slightly protruding between her top and bottom teeth. There it was, just for me.

"Remember that month I made you abstain?" she eventually asked, forcing *thistle* back into hiding.

I pretended to search my mind for something seared right into my forehead from fourteen years prior.

"Not really ringing a bell...."

"Aw, stop making me feel bad."

"What I remember is the day it ended."

"Boy, I do too. I'm sorry I put you through all that. I just...sex was so new to me, to us, and I had to be sure you loved me and not just the sex. You just went with it, handled it with such cool maturity."

"Let's not dwell on what I handled, shall we?"

Maezie fought to suppress the grin growing on her face as I carried on.

"I don't know if I ever properly thanked you. I mean, I bought stock in Jergens that first day at eleven and sold it thirty days later at eighty-seven and a half."

Her laughter filled the hotel room.

"Now you're just rubbing it in."

"Don't talk to me about rubbing it, woman. Didn't you think it odd that I suddenly became obsessed with the callouses on my hands, more specifically, my left hand? My poor Mama never did get her pumice stone back."

Maezie gasped for air. "Stop it! You are just too funny."

Over the next hour, we sat on the edge of the bed and talked about sex, discussing the pros and cons of giving in to our passions like two spirits floating above their own funerals, two sports commentators analyzing the options for the underdogs in the final minutes of play, two star-crossed lovers all-too aware of how the story was going to end. We both wanted each other so very badly, but it all came down to the fact that neither of us could live with ourselves if we put our own selfish needs above the other, innocent players, waiting in the wings for the leads to get their shit together, for the director to say, "And scene." We'd already soiled any remaining purity of her union, and that was hard enough to contend with, but to commit "the act" would be the death knell, ultimately uprooting the lives of innocent children. We had to fight that with all the will power we could muster. We both knew once wasn't going to scratch the itch. It would ignite the craving for that once-in-a-lifetime love we had.

We were fools then and masochists now.

"All right," Maezie finally declared. "I need to go to bed. The conference starts at eight, but I'll be free by one, so we can grab lunch somewhere before I head out. Where are you staying tonight?"

That question had never entered my mind.

"I assumed here, with you."

"Oh, no. That's a bad plan...a very bad plan."

"Okay. Well, I'll just check with the front desk or head to the Omni or something."

Maezie didn't want me to go, and I didn't want to leave, but she was one hundred percent right. Me staying the night was tantamount to throwing gasoline on the bonfire that was already raging out of control. I sat on the bed and made a production out of putting on my shoes.

"Fine! You can stay. But you keep your clothes on, *and* you sleep on top of the covers."

"Yes, ma'am."

Maezie opened her suitcase and extracted the cutest Nick & Nora strawberry print pajamas.

"Sneaky shit. I know you planned this."

"Me?"

She pointed at my crotch. *"Him."*

"I'll deal with him later," I promised.

"After I'm gone, please," Maezie lectured as she made for the bathroom to change. "You better not be naked when I get back...."

It took every bit of fortitude to pull back on the reins, but I was true to my word that night.

For her part, Maezie held my hand (on top of the covers), and we slept like babies.

The next morning, I had a moment of weakness while I was showering. Maezie was at the desk in our room applying her makeup, and I thought of simply exiting the bathroom and dropping my towel and ravaging her, morals be damned, but an angel watching over me swooped in to help me deal with a suddenly clogged toilet. I'll say no more because it just doesn't belong in my, or any, epic tale of romance. Although it ended up being funny as hell.

Suffice it to say, we managed to get the hell out of the hotel room without doing "the deed," and I managed to find something to do for the next several hours while Maezie attended her boring-ass conference. I doubled back to the gift shop and bought the earrings and, yes, I bought the damn rooster and paid to have it shipped home. As if she needed anything further to remember that weekend by.

I don't remember our goodbye that afternoon, probably because we both knew that we'd exhausted every possible "safe" avenue for our renewed acquaintance, and all that shit had to come to a screeching halt. What I do remember was that it was the greatest people watching experience of my life at the IHOP where we ate our final meal together. There was something truly special about having maple syrup come out your nose. It topped Swiss Miss, I'll tell you that much.

For the first time since Puerto Vallarta, Maezie made the foo dog face, but not because the food was bad. She was choking briefly at one point. Talking/eating/laughing was a bad combo.

I have no idea what was so entertaining that afternoon, but every damn patron in that place fell victim to our running commentary. It made for one helluva memorable sendoff as the clock ran down to zero.

God, did we laugh.

31

A Walk to Forget

I'm too ashamed to make a written record of what Javi and I did at the Seva chocolate factory, but let's just say that all their fancy packaging was completely lost on us. Our gracious hosts offered samples to illustrate the process of making this type of chocolate treat and that, and I wanted the entire coffee table book. I handed the owner a hundred bucks and told him to shit samples all over us—pardon the analogy—and if I had any change at the end of the process, we'd deal with it then.

I was doing a decent job of eating and drinking away my sorrows, but I was more than a little upset with Maezie for bailing on me. For starters, she was missing out on some mighty special chocolate-smeared kisses. Plus, I looked pretty rakish in my new hat which I hadn't managed to lose yet.

Yay, me....

"That's enough for today, Javi," I moaned in the direction of my new best bud when we arrived back at the van.

"Fuck, yeah, it is" Javi moaned back, his delivery reminding me of one of Maezie's well-timed f-bombs, and I laughed loud and hearty.

"I hope you and Elena have a good time with the chocolate tonight. I imagine that is pretty far up on her craving list these days."

"It is, for sure, but I do not believe I will be joining her. You will score big with her for this generous gift, though."

"Glad to do it, buddy. I've had a really good time today. Thank you for taking me around and sharing all this cool shit. It's been awesome, and I love my new hat."

"Yes, it makes you look quite important."

"Like a fucking drug lord is what I hear you saying."

"Perhaps. But the boss of the bosses."

"The boss of the bosses. I'll take that."

"I will drop you at the front of the hotel. If I come inside, they may beg me to work, and I am too full. I need to rest!"

"You've earned it, my friend. Just pull up anywhere and toss me out. I'm headed straight to the room for a nap and may not show my face again until breakfast. And even then, I think I'll stick with the melon."

"Okay," Javi said, acknowledging our mutually pitiful state with a pat of his belly.

He oozed back behind the wheel, and after another quiet, ten-minute journey, we pulled up in front of the hotel.

"Here you are. Have a restful evening."

"You, too, Javi." I shook his hand and pulled myself from the van. "I'll see you tomorrow sometime. Take care."

"Very good, señor. See you then. Good night."

"Night."

"Aw, hell, it's 1:00 a.m.," I told myself after finally locating my phone in the dark. Not that I had anywhere at all to be, but that little nap I was gonna take had turned into a full-fledged five hours of sleep, and now I'd messed up whatever internal clock I'd had going on before the chocolate gorging session.

I opened the mini fridge to get a beer and there was all the stuff for Chicken Pontalba staring me in the face. Shit. I needed to do something with that. Maybe dinner tomorrow, if I had the will, or the energy.

Shit, Maezie. Why am I such a fucking dumbass?

And then it was 3:42 a.m.

I'd been watching local television with the sound off, lost in the harsh reality that was closing in on me from all sides.

What the hell am I even still doing here?

Maezie said she wasn't coming, and I knew she wasn't, because at least one person had to be responsible in this relationship, and it sure as hell wasn't me.

Stupid. *Fucking stupid.*

"Make a damn plan, Kenzie!"

I could easily stay in Ecuador. Not this trip, but I could easily retire here at some point. It's been beautiful, and money has gone a long way in these parts. Maezie was one hundred percent right about that. But, staying here much longer on this current excursion would only drive me insane, wrestling with my conscience no matter what tours and distractions Javi and I got ourselves into. Best to book a flight back home and get the hell out, I reasoned. *Maybe someday, if I outlive Hubby #3 or he pulls some stupid shit like his predecessor, I'll finally get my turn at bat.*

A guy can dream....

Okay, I decided. One more day in Paradise Lost, and I'd pack it up. The plan was to get up—I mean, I was wide awake— and slip on my linen drawstring pants, which were wrinkled to hell and back and caked in sand all over the cuffs, but it was dark out and nobody cared anyway. A walk on the beach sounded relaxing, and the odds were in my favor that I wouldn't encounter Mr. and Mrs. Hammock at that early hour. I'd take my beer and go dip my feet in the ocean, feel the breeze. Wash out my brain.

Yeah. *Good luck with that last one.*

There was just enough moon to see where I was going, and I had the beach to myself. The pounding of the surf worked hard to drown out my negative thoughts, and the water felt nice on my feet. It was definitely one of the better ideas I've had since I've been down here.

CIRCLE BACK

• • •

A few weeks after our return from San Antonio, Maezie's school started back up. I got busy with a flurry of work but did make a memorable early morning visit to Kilgore in September to give her the gold earrings she'd had her eye on, which made her happy. Sadly, the rooster had arrived at Casa Church in 409 pieces, so that surprise went straight into the trash bin.

The mutual feeling of shame overshadowed our encounter and made the rendezvous feel cheap somehow, and I was glad the rooster had bitten the dust. It would've been too much.

We were just reaching the point of saying goodbye for what I assumed would be another healthy stretch when who should round the corner in his Lincoln but Mr. Potter himself.

Maezie saw him coming first and told me in even tones to nod and shake her hand, get in my Jeep and drive away. I did as instructed and left her to cover our tracks as best she could.

I learned later that I was "just a parent" making routine inquiries. But he had a jealous side and any encounter between his wife and another man was bad news according to Maezie. Maybe his gut instinct had also been on high alert, and I wasn't giving him enough credit. In any case, he began screening her mail and monitoring her calls, which only hastened our decision to cool our jets while we still could.

I left Maezie alone until the following May when my birthday rolled around. I risked a morning drive-by at the school but had the sense to remain in my car and simply intercept her in the parking lot. We had two minutes of catch-up before the Lincoln came into view once more.

"I can't keep doing this, Kenzie," she said with anger emerging in her eyes. "I'm sorry."

And that was the last I saw or heard from Maezie for the next twenty-five years.

We left each other alone, she to raise her family, and me to try and find someone to start a life with and build a family of my own.

I reached out to her only once during that interim period, in the form of an email in 2007 during a particularly rough patch in my three-year-old marriage. I simply said that I thought of her often and still loved her and missed her.

For my trouble, my wife came across that email, and the rough patch evolved into a sizeable pothole. Maezie told me recently she never got the email in question. For at the time, she and Mr. Potter were going through their own rough patch and, as she put it, "Had I received it, I probably would've left him."

I'm not sure her wishy-washy theoretical pronouncement qualified as anything, so I simply tucked it into the memory box in my mind with all our other coulda woulda shouldas.

My marriage survived another fifteen years and the raising of my own precious child.

Maezie claimed to have imagined me happy, so she didn't reach out when she and Mr. Potter finally called it quits. Her daughter from her first marriage eventually set Maezie up on a date with an old high school flame, who'd recently divorced, and within a year or two, they married and settled in Fort Worth.

I came back on the market early in 2022 after being traded in for a younger model. I didn't blame Not Maezie. My heart and that other part hadn't been in it to win it for a long while, and the first thing I did was exhaust the internet trying to find where my Maezie had gone.

She no longer taught school, and the trail had gone cold. But upon Judd's passing, I'd inherited the historic images and recordings of the Louisiana Hayride and spent many years earning a living as an archivist. If I knew anything, it was how to research. I saw where Maezie had landed after she remarried, but it had been a number of years, so maybe....

And that's where this whole story began for you, dear reader.

Meanwhile, there I was, strolling a beautiful beach in a beautiful part of the world, thinking about a beautiful woman that was once mine.

So much for my walk to forget.

32

Once More with Feeling

My darling Maezie,

In my youth, I prayed to God for you long before I ever knew you existed. I asked of my Savior that I may come to find a piece of me I sensed was missing; that I may come to know a singular and beautiful, deep and far-reaching soul-altering experience that would prepare me in some way for the goodness of Heaven. Much sooner than I was prepared to handle, he sent you into my life—a beautiful dandelion whose blowball exploded all over my world when I blew love into it. I was totally blinded by your splendor and left searching for a way to repay the riches I was sure I did not deserve.

What you and I came to find in one another was divine, not of this Earth. And it came so easily that I failed to see its worth, failed to shield us from the routine attacks of this mortal world and our fragile human nature. When we collapsed under the strains and demands we'd placed on our union—on my watch!—I simply let it tear us apart. I have grieved every moment of every day of every decade since.

I was a boy charged with making the decisions of a man. I failed that man, and I failed you.

Maezie, my angel, what I could not know then, and what I've only recently come to see, is the rarest of love you and I shared those many years ago has continued to grow and mature in some otherworldly space. A great fog of misery rolled in and eclipsed our existence, or so we thought, but what we grieved was never lost, only our ability to see it.

I came here to Ecuador to live out the dream scarcely out of your mouth, for it came from a place I was desperate to find once more. Here, I have relived every precious moment and every painful one, and only now have I paused to consider how great the album of our shared lives has truly been. Though our paths have failed to line up in the many years since college, our aim and direction has stayed true, and the experience I asked God for has been in no way slighted. Everything happens in His time for a reason, and His ways are not always for us to know or understand.

Today, I find I am weary of staring at defeat, of mourning another missed opportunity, of hiding in shame for trying to force fate. And in my misery, I choose to flip the coin over and see the blinding beauty that has remained steadfast all these years.

We have such great glory in our history, Maezie, a bounty of incalculable value. I knew when my marriage was ending that you'd be there to catch me, and that drove me hard to take back the love that should've always been mine. But in this quiet early morning, I'm smiling through my tears because I have seen for myself that the love I seek has not vacated my life. I have spent years trying to take back something that never left. I was the one who ran from it all when my place, my obligation, my duty as a sentinel was to stand guard over our precious love until we meet in the Hereafter.

Live your best life, my love, and know, always, I am with you. I'm there when you need a friend, there when you stumble. There when you laugh yourself silly, and when you land the perfect f-bomb at the most imperfect of moments. Thank you for being the part of me I can never wear down; the ear deaf to criticism; the spirit that cannot be defeated.

Know always that we share a heart. That we alone occupy the deep end of the pool, unafraid to swim and delight there for all time. You are irreplaceable in my heart, Maezie, a yardstick I have foolishly used to measure others by and will no doubt do so for the rest of my days.

I guess what I'm trying to say is I'm here with you all the time and wish you every happiness. The boy you knew is perhaps now a man, and he will resume his post as guardian over the greatest treasure. If your heart skips a beat, I will know it. If it stops, I will start it again. Our world is not here in Ecuador or there in Fort Worth or New Orleans, but in that timeless space, in our hearts forever.

You will never know how much you've enriched my life and my very soul, but each day, in your quiet time, I will try and tell you through the ether.

*Eternally Yours,
Kenzie*

33

Una Cariñosa Despedida

The day, the time, and the hour of my departure has arrived. I've done all I can do in this foreign coastal space, except torture my soul further.

But enough already.

I gave the chicken and fixings to the restaurant to do as they please. I said my goodbyes to Grandpa Munster and Sting and did my best to settle accounts with Maezie through a heartfelt email. I'll head back to New Orleans now and rest a bit, maybe go surprise my daughter at college to see how she's getting along. I could use one of her hugs, and she'll know how to coach me back to sanity without sounding defeatist or letting me get too bogged down in feeling sorry for myself. Smart one, that kiddo of mine.

Javi did his best yesterday to distract me and help round out my understanding of this beautiful place that

Johnny Veenci first told me of all those eons ago. We took in the rainforest, a coffee plantation, and both local museums. I tell ya, if anything related to this country ever comes up on any future editions of *Drunk*—or *Sober*—*Jeopardy*, I'll most certainly kick some serious ass.

I give one more look around Room 5 and slip $40 under my pillow for the housekeeping staff. My flight leaves at 3:20 p.m. Time to grab a cab and go.

I finally spot my partner in crime, the esteemed Javier Fortunato Edgarto Quishpe, aka Quito, aka Javi, emerging from the lobby.

He seems distracted.

I nab his attention with a wave as I approach. "Well, amigo, I guess this is it. Time for me to ease on down the road. But I'll be back, Javi, you know I will. I want to meet Elena and that coming attraction of yours. And who knows, maybe next time, the tour will be through neighborhoods, real estate for sale."

"Something tells me I will be seeing you very soon."

We fall into a hug that pushes the boundaries of allowable macho-ness—his more than mine—but I pull back, nonetheless, for a final look at my good friend as I reach into my pocket. I want to help this guy. I want to make a difference in his life.

"Aren't you forgetting something, Señor Kenzie?"

Jeez. Give me half a second, Javi. I'm gonna do the right thing here. "No, no, Javi. There's no way I can ever thank or repay you for your service, kindness, and friendship, but all the same.... Gimme a second, willya?"

My words trail off as I shift focus to the wad of cash in my hand and begin counting. *What the fuck, he deserves the whole thing.* In my shame, in my defeat, my eyes remain downcast, and a tear drops onto my wrist as I pretend to keep counting.

Shit. *Hand him the money, mumble something, and be gone, Kenzie. Go!*

"Here. You and Elena need anything at all, you call me or email." I tuck a biz card into his breast pocket. "Stay in touch. I mean that."

As I move to deliver the cash, Javi stops me with a hands-up gesture of *no* as his face explodes into the biggest smile I've ever seen—gums over teeth by two to one, easy. A Barbie pink sunset over a white sand beach.

I don't understand this feeling of unbridled joy, so out of place is it in my world of misery that my eyes return to the concrete. I search my recent memory banks for things I may've left behind. I reflexively reach for my head. Nope, the not-from-Panama hat's securely in place. Got my cell phone. My damn wallet's in my hand, and the driver, who's pulled up, is out and stowing the suitcase in the trunk of my ride.

I feel another hug erupting, so I insert a foot into the cab and do the head tuck to get in when a flash of red inserts itself into my periphery. It feels familiar. Untucking and straightening up, I see Javi's head tilt almost imperceptibly right where the energy bomb is exploding in my eyeline.

"Oh, hello," Maezie offers as she strolls up to us in those sexy-as-hell lipstick-red shoes from forty-plus years ago. The gal has always known how to make an entrance, I'm tellin' ya.

The calendar of my mind says it's September 5, 1980, a little after eight in the evening. Her eyes confirm the time warp as our memories merge to create a singular newfound reality.

"Hello, yourself," I offer back. (And for the purpose of this glorious ending, I sound nothing like a croaking toad.)

Maezie shoots Javi a dutiful but sincere closed-mouthed smile, and then takes my hands in hers, those Egyptian eyes locked like a magnet on my cloudy ones as she escorts us back toward the Hotel Vistalmar. My thoughts are hopelessly out of sync with my eyes and emotions. I can't seem to process the magnitude of this moment. Maezie. Here? Now?

I've failed in my efforts to describe that first magical college kiss, this I know. But let me say this, faithful reader, in some small offering of consolation....

The kiss that followed the reunion of Maezie and Kenzie in Ecuador was a greater statement than the one on the patio of a college dive bar wrought with hormones, and greater than the one in San Antonio that was swimming in heartache. It was the perfect bookend to our story. We had, in fact, circled back as promised. Walls of bright red and yellow, that broken ArklaGas grill, scattered picnic tables, cheap beer, and that lilting laugh from the girl with the Florence Henderson haircut—*LDM*— all those memories came flooding back in that instant.

"*Cara Mia,*" seeped from my lips as I pulled away to ensure by way of the most dominant sense that the moment was real.

Semaphore signals, our own special code, answered all remaining questions.

Her mouth rested open in the most charming position, tongue pushing between the rows of perfectly white teeth. And then....

Thistle.

34

The Baroness

"Aren't you forgetting something, Señor Kenzie?" I said to Javi in the worst possible imitation of his little bullshit line as soon as I'd emerged from the reunion with Maezie on that exceedingly memorable day at Hotel Vistalmar. *"Something tells me I will be seeing you very soon,"* my mockery continued and was rewarded with a giant smile and a blameless shrug.

"I was told to keep my mouth shut," Javi offered in his meager defense.

I turned back to Maezie and found her laughing. I kissed her teeth and, eventually, her lips as we renewed our vain attempt to make up for lost time.

"And I was told the lady is hungry from her journey, so with your permission, Señor Kenzie, I should like to serve the happy couple with a special meal on the patio."

"Love. Honor. Cherish," Maezie counted out on her fingers. "And Feed."

Her eyes. Those long-lost crescents. Mine forever. Nothing else mattered.

"Yeah...sure. By all means," was my response to Javi's outstretched hand and Maezie's beautiful smile.

Javi showed us to my usual table where I delighted in pulling Maezie's chair out for her.

"That's Sting, and that's Grandpa Munster," I said by way of introduction to the two tyrannulet birds observing our placement below them.

"Oh, how funny!" Maezie brightened. "You weren't kidding."

Maezie took in the beautiful setting as I sat down opposite her, clasped both her hands in mine, and just outright stared in disbelief. I had questions, and she had answers, but it could all wait. I kissed her hands one at a time, but quickly, as I didn't want to break eye contact lest she disappear. I felt a fullness inside as my chest struggled to contain my swelling heart. Maezie loosed a tear, and I wasn't far behind. So much had to be said and was said in the long silence that followed.

"And here you are," Javi offered as he appeared tableside, shocking us back to the present with his delivery. "A special meal for a very special day."

Javi delivered the two gorgeous plates, then stood back awaiting our reaction.

I spoke first because I knew what he had done. "Perfect," I offered in a low tone as I returned his extra-large smile.

"Looks amazing," Maezie commented. "What is it?"

"I believe you know it as Chicken Pontalba," Javi said with pride. "It was Señor Kenzie's idea."

Maezie smiled bright and beautiful when it dawned on her. A healthy bite ensued.

"This is amazing," she declared to the two men ogling her as she ate.

Javi nodded and seemed genuinely touched as he bowed and prepared to exit. "Most excellent. Enjoy."

"Micaela, Baroness de Pontalba," Maezie shared with me after another savory bite of the chicken. "I got an A on that stupid paper thanks to you. Lord, I haven't thought about her in years."

"I hope it makes up for the polo dirt."

"Oh, God, is that what this is about?!" Maezie replied through fingers working to keep her latest bite inside her open mouth. "You are too funny, Mackenzie Church."

I watched as some sort of wave passed over Maezie, some realization that had been triggered by the utterance of my name, said this time with total freedom.

"Pretty good, huh?" I inquired after finally taking my first bite.

"The best," she eventually whispered.

35

Denouement

After our late lunch, Maezie asked that we just sit in silence for a while, and I was more than happy to oblige. We found our way to the beach and huddled like two members of a bobsled team, minus the bobsled, watching the sunset from a sandy berm. And life was perfect.

I kissed her neck, inhaled her fragrance, and thanked God for the miracle of having her once more in my arms. We held each other just as we had so long ago, and the feeling of total possession was exhilarating. Waves crashed and receded. *You two*, I heard my mother say. Bliss.

"Come and sit beside me," Maezie said as she worked to untangle and reposition us. The time had come to talk. She took my hands in hers and our eyes darted back and forth, studying and anticipating. "I love you, Mackenzie," she said with piercing resolution.

I opened my mouth to speak but was silenced by her finger to my lips and a slight shake side to side that told me to wait my turn.

After a moment, she continued. "You and I failed each other all those many years ago. We can't have those years back, and that hurts like hell, but we have to accept our choices and our stupidity. We were dumb kids, Kenzie. We didn't know better. Wasn't your fault, wasn't mine. We just didn't know.

"I searched for you in every partner I've known in all the years since. I've raised precious children and had moments of great joy and happiness. But I've also experienced darkness and pain and illness like no one should ever know. I've known love and felt love but what I feel when I hear your voice or read your texts or, my God, see you in person...."

Maezie struggled to continue, eventually finding her footing again. "That feeling is so very *different*." She broke our grip on each other to wipe her eyes, and I did the same.

"Number Three really is a lot like you. My daughter set us up because she thought an old flame from high school might make me happy again. And he was...*is* a good man. And we had a lot of good times together, but we'd settled into separate lives long before you came back into the picture. For me, marriage is a routine I've long grown used to, Kenz, a marathon with water breaks along the way. A marathon I became determined to win."

Maezie searched my eyes for the words she needed to say or the permission to say them, I'm not sure which. She took my face in her hands and kissed my cheeks, eyes, and lips before continuing.

"No one does *that* to me," she said as she clutched her heart. "That's because you own this and always have. All those stupid-ass debates we had about cheating—it was done the first moment we strayed from each other. Had nothing to do with *the act*."

I managed a nod of agreement.

"Last week, my daughter, same one, said to me, '*You should see the way you light up when he texts you.*' Boy, you really made an impression on that one! Then Javier called me...."

"*Javi?!*"

A nod. "You passed out on your journal, phone open."

"That sneaky bastard."

"Oh, the man painted quite the portrait of misery, Kenz. He should get an award for that performance. Then I got your goodbye email and thought, you know, what the hell am I doing? Martyring oneself for a defunct marriage or some clothing store is the same stupid fucking thing."

Maezie stopped talking and her words just seemed to hang there.

I began to nod as everything came crashing into place.

"My commitment is to you, Mackenzie Church, and to us. I want to spend the rest of my life with you. That's why I'm here."

A pause, then a kiss to seal the deal.

"Now it's your turn," she muttered, pulling back from our hungry kiss.

"You've been the yardstick in my love life from the very first moment I met you, Maezie. You are the center of my compass, and it is with all the maturity and wisdom I'm ever gonna have that I commit my heart and soul to you and to us for always. You are forever mine, in this life and the next. I love you with all my heart."

More kissing. Waves crashed and receded round the world. Trust me, they did.

"You and me," Maezie softly replied. "Period."

Postscriptum

"Wait!" Maezie commands as I stack our breakfast plates along an arm. "I need to poke some holes in it."

She stabs the banana slice we'd reserved for our "guests" with a fork.

"Carry on," she allows upon completion of the task to her satisfaction.

I somehow pull off the balancing act and make it to the table in the conservatory without incident. Maezie follows with our juice glasses and a fistful of napkins. Together, we decant my armload and take our seats. Maezie places the remains of the banana on a shelf near the open transom. We don't have long to wait.

"Well, good morning, Bruce." Maezie smiles at the butterfly flitting about the fruit. "Or is that Rod?" she asks, lathering cream cheese on her mini bagel.

"Right the first time," I assure her. "Bruce is the black swallowtail with the yellow dots. Rod is the ruby one. Just remember—"

"Or," Maezie interjects, "we could just file the whole thing under *Who Gives a Shit?*"

Mango juice out the nostrils punctuates my delight at the woman who has always had impeccable timing.

"Or that," I agree right before back-to-back sneezes expel the last of the orange-colored elixir and reduce Maezie to a fit of silent laughter.

Yes, I became a butterfly rancher in my golden years. Sort of.

Satisfied?

Maezie and I finally got our place in Colorado, a beautiful cabin in the woods just below Ouray, and we split our time between there and our beach house in Manta.

Javi and Elena remain very much a part of our lives. I backed Javi in his tour business, and the man built it into an empire that extends all over northern Ecuador. And Mazie and I became the proud godparents of "baby Lia," who is currently graduating from high school.

Where does the time go?

"C'mon, old man," Maezie lectures. "Tonight's steak night, so we gotta get our walking in early. You know me after a glass of wine."

"Or two."

"Or three, funny man. Yes, I know you do. Got the keys?"

"Right here," I say, giving them a jingle as proof.

And with that, Maezie takes my hand in hers and we head on our daily walk, just one of the routines we've settled into in this wonderful world of our making. We're that old Italian couple walking along hand in hand in silence. (Only we're German and Scottish and other things, and we both talk up a storm.) We're intertwined, one heart, one unit.

And grateful for each other.

Perhaps that's the greatest thing I can say about Kenzie and Maezie Church, husband and wife for going on eighteen years now. All the velvet ropes are gone. All the sheets are off the furniture, and all the rooms of our collective mansion are teeming with life once more. Our children are supportive, and our grandkids are delightful pains in our one big ass. We live in the deep end, totally committed to each other, and for all our faults, we love each other, deeply and unconditionally.

It is possible, you know.

CIRCLE BACK

Made in United States
Orlando, FL
07 December 2024